Ruth Plant grew up in a country vicarage in Staffordshire in the early years of this century, a period now looked back to nostalgically as one of security and comfort. She draws a subtle, memorable picture of herself as a child and of the world around her, a world which was to change for ever after the end of the First World War.

BEYOND THE NURSERY WINDOW

Ruth Plant tells of her youth in a country vicarage in Staffordshire early in this century, a story she began in her earlier book NANNY AND I. Together with the occasional dip back into childhood memories of a nursery kingdom where Nanny reigned supreme, she ventures forth into a world of schooldays and visits to relatives, the exciting world of London and the theatre, the wonders of Bath and the beauties of the Lake District. She travels to Oberammergau, and sees Hitler on a visit there. On the threshold of life the future seems bright and war far away.

Books by Ruth Plant
Published by The House of Ulverscroft:

NANNY AND I

RUTH PLANT

BEYOND THE NURSERY WINDOW

Complete and Unabridged

ULVERSCROFT
Leicester

First published in Great Britain in 1985

First Large Print Edition
published 1999

British Library CIP Data

Plant, Ruth, *1909 – 1997*
    Beyond the nursery window.—Large print ed.—
Ulverscroft large print series: non-fiction
1. Plant, Ruth, *1909 – 1997*
2. Women—England—Biography
3. Children—England—Biography
4. Large type books
5. England—Social life and customs—20th
century
I. Title
942′.083′092

ISBN 0–7089–4068–4

Published by
F. A. Thorpe (Publishing) Ltd.
Anstey, Leicestershire
Set by Words & Graphics Ltd.
Anstey, Leicestershire
Printed and bound in Great Britain by
T. J. International Ltd., Padstow, Cornwall

This book is printed on acid-free paper

1

On Opening a Box of Doll's Clothes

It was opening the old box that did it. First, it was the scent of things which is a marvellous activator of memory. That indefinable mixture of smells which resembles no known mixture in the list of famous perfumiers, but which has a subtlety of its own.

I was back in the world of childhood, in the security of the nursery with Nanny sitting by the shaded oil lamp working at a new smock for me, and my brother in his dressing gown chuckling over some recent joke in the *Boy's Own Paper*.

Then there was the feel of the clothes, too, that brought so much back to memory, the rough serge of Big Doll's navy jacket that seemed almost to prick the fingers. It was a short coat edged with white braid, an attempt at a sailor jacket perhaps, like my brother wore for best occasions and family photographs; owing to lack of stuff, it being just an odd piece left over from another garment, it had ended up something like a bolero.

1

There was that fine white ninon, held together by a firm yoke of double material, as so many frocks were in those days, with some feather-stitching round it; a confirmation dress I thought it, not that Big Doll ever got confirmed, but as a parson's daughter I had attended many of these functions and been very much impressed by them at that early age.

Seeing it now reminded me of my own confirmation dress, created many years later to be worn among a bevy of rather critical schoolgirls, a heavy expensive edition of *crêpe de chine* which was revered more for its material value than the light ethereal beauty of Big Doll's ninon. When my frock had come from the local dressmakers (since it was not so easy to get a suitable frock readymade), people who called and saw it immediately felt it between their fingers, its thickness was such as almost to give the impression of a grained material, and it was pronounced very good and different from the slippery shininess of Jap silk which was mainly used for linings. Its only ornament was some gathering, especially at the waist, but I personally felt rather weighed down by its physical and visual heaviness and at a time when I was to appear in it somewhat in the public eye it did little to help my schoolgirl self-consciousness. The only saving grace was the large sleeves which widened as they went on, giving me an air of elegance and an ample covering for red schoolgirl hands.

I recall how its severity had contrasted with the frocks I saw later on our holiday in St Mâlo when we happened later to spend Whitsun in Brittany. The French had that flair for the feminine that caused them to create little frills and chic touches, so that it was almost like a dance parade when they lined up for the Bishop. No wonder people thought of it as something of a show and climbed irreverently on the side altars, from which they were ruthlessly swept by a large beadle in an embroidered frock coat, armed with a huge staff rather like a mace: a secular bureaucrat he looked to us but employed by a spiritual organisation.

Even the boys too were specially dressed for this event wearing rather feminine looking sailor suits with enormous white bows on their coat at the side to match the white sailor collar. The bow had great long ends that hung down below their waists. To add to this opportunity for display they paraded the streets in these garments. How strange to see on the rather grubby and realistic quay of Cancale for instance, with fishing boats lined up ready for the away, loaded with greasy tackle and winches, these visions of pure white picking their way between all the slippery mud left by the incoming catches.

Then my mind went to Vienna where the young candidates were paraded about not on foot, but in coaches with open hoods lined with crudely dyed birds' feathers in shell shape, making it seem more like a cabaret.

Big Doll did not only have a confirmation dress, however. Her wardrobe was really quite considerable because she was an important member of the doll family. It was her size and her face that most impressed me at that time. The latter was tastefully painted with a bright rosy shade almost like a blush on her cheeks. Her eyes were big and childlike with pale blue pupils. Her hair, had you looked at it with a critical eye, was rather like a poor quality wig with the parting disclosing how firmly it was glued to the foundations, but to my childlike scrutiny she appeared only a flaxen-haired girl of a romantic story-book type.

However, she was really a Goss Doll, a family of china manufacturers whose young people I was to know in later years but I never connected them with making famous dolls. It was strange that unlike the other dolls she never acquired an individual name. I think some were tried out from time to time but they never stuck indicating that she was an impressive ornament rather than a personality like the other more human ones of lesser status. It was understandable that she finally ended up for auction at Sothebys in spite of a broken china leg.

Nanny had also made her a frock in a rose pink material with a lovely embroidery on the yoke, of a bunch of flowers; there was a hat too and that had a large sunflower worked on it. She was the only doll who was presented with a hat but it was not a very successful one. The brim consisted of a cut-out of round cardboard with a piece of the dress material gathered round it, but as it was not supported by any stiffening in the crown it flapped about either being right off her face or over her eyes; in vain did I try to get it to stand out like my hat brims did. But then why should we expect Nanny to be a milliner as well as a dressmaker? So Big Doll did not often wear the hat; it was nice after all to show off flaxen hair, and there was that splendid bunch of daisies that Nanny had embroidered on her yoke. All dresses seemed to have yokes and if they did not then the gap must be filled up by the modesty vest. In an age when most mothers fed their babies naturally the bosom was I suppose the focus of womanhood and this was why people made so much of it.

The next in the social order was Gloria. Her name alone gave her status. She was called after the grand-daughter of a titled friend of ours who lived in a castle, and whose grandfather on the other side of the family was a famous actor.

Gloria was the opposite in colouring to Big Doll, being a brunette, with dark hair possibly real but stitched on rather clumsily to avoid it blowing away. Her eyes were of a deeper blue. Her frock too was of a sharper pink and a more sophisticated material, rather a springy one a little like an alpaca. It must have been difficult for Nanny to sew but in spite of this Gloria even had a matching coat over her frock in a rather tailored style, and decorated with some beautiful buttons, the rims of which were silver. What's more, they fastened in a strange way into the back of the material with a little clasp you twisted round. How fond I was of those buttons with the shiny rims. Unusual clips at the back for holding them in place seemed something unique to me.

Gloria had rather a lavish supply of underwear, too, which gave one the feeling of having a high class wardrobe and made her softer to cuddle too.

Then there was Baby Boy, a perfectly jointed doll with wonderfully bendable limbs to fit into the elaborate woollen layette provided for him by the donor, my very liberal godmother. She had knitted all the garments herself. He was very pink and white with a realistic head of curls to look at from afar. It was not till you got near that you realised that his head was wholly china and the curls painted on with slight indentations in the moulding to enhance reality.

There were old friends, too, among the dolls, such as Ivy in her green cape made from a bit of my dress and the white Vyella frock smocked like mine with a big pink ribbon bow near the yoke with its ends hanging down lavishly. It was coming across that frock that carried me back most vividly perhaps because it was so constantly used when I played with those dolls. Ivy was such an old friend.

There were also the dolls that I inherited from relatives not such personal friends but interesting additions to my collection. Penelope, for instance, whose body was entirely made of white kid and had even a built-in bustle and a tiny waist and glorious blue eyes with a glassy look and flowing fair hair that seemed real and needed to be tied up with ribbon to keep it tidy. Susan, the doll given me by Aunt Nellie, had a most elaborate Victorian hairstyle, with little curls and a fringe, but like Baby Boy's it was all part of her china head really which made it seem rather remote to me, but at least the curls did not get out of place like Penelope's real hair. She was rather small but very slim and chic and her red suit was of woollen material beautifully tailored with puff sleeves and decorated with lace.

Aunt Nellie, though a fierce member of the family with whom I had little contact, was the origin of some important gifts, especially her Dolls' House. What a whole new world opened for me when I sat down in front of that fascinating object, and moved the exquisite furniture which made it all seem so real. Even the kitchen pots were there for the solid cook in starched apron to place on the old black range ready for dinner.

Its exterior was typically Victorian, though there was a hint of the Georgian influence in the long thin windows that in a real house would have had sashes, and the porch was supported by white classical columns that matched the over-hanging cornice that ran along the front of the roof.

The rest of the facade was of rather crude red brick, painted on with clear white 'pointing' in between each brick that made it stand out. The large windows were hung with lace which had obviously been intended for a petticoat flounce, but hung sideways it made excellent lace curtains to cover the big windows discreetly, leaving one to imagine what went on behind them.

The front door was of a solid dark brown with panels painted on it and an impressive door handle. One expected it to swing back at any moment and reveal an obsequious butler or a uniformed parlour maid, but instead you had to move out the whole front having undone the hook at the side, and there stood revealed all the four rooms at once, a breathtaking sight.

Naturally one migrated to the dining room first because it was on the ground floor and had the best furniture. There was an exquisite suite of furniture in shining black with some gold decorations. There were two chairs with arms, obviously for the host and hostess, at opposite ends of the table and some matching uprights for the guests, or the family. They were all upholstered in exquisite mauve taffeta which toned in wonderfully.

The dining table was perhaps of a later period in a dark brown mahogany, with fluted edges and rounded corners which gave it an individual style. There was a sideboard which matched it, but it was rather tall. Realistic touches had been added, like a huge dish of plastic grapes and a Sheffield

Plate cover for any hot dish brought in. The only drawback was that these dishes were so heavy they were apt to topple the high sideboard, and it would come crashing down away from the wall which was covered by a typical Victorian wallpaper of dark red with an elaborate pattern worked out in a darker shade. The same problem occurred with the kitchen dresser next door and it seemed difficult to tie it to the wall. It was full of things that hung on pegs all waiting to be used for some elaborate meals. The old black kitchen range with an oven and a boiler was set back in an embrasure in the wall with a wide mantelpiece high up on which a clock stood to ensure punctuality. There was even a coal bucket ready to keep the range refuelled.

The drawing room was upstairs, and had something of the romantic frills that drawing rooms had in those days, with a paler wallpaper to match them, but I seem to recall that I must have put in some Edwardian additions because the sofa which was rather more cushioned and cosy than the stern austerity that the Victorians allowed themselves in seating, was covered in shadow tissue, the inevitable choice for vicarage drawing rooms in those days, when I lived in one. There were also some pictures on the wall in keeping with this mood of a romantic garden scene with roses rather resembling those on the sofa cushions but with a big stone pedestal and vase in the middle of the scene. I have an idea it had come to us as a Christmas card and been cut down for further use. That was why it would never stay in its frame properly and was a source of constant annoyance. Strangely enough I have it still, and the jacket design of this book is based on it. The other pictures, an etching of a romantic scene and the famous Landseer of two dogs in a kennel, completed the decorations to the wall.

The bedroom next door had everything including a varnished washstand in light wood with a round hole in the top to exactly fit the little white china washbasin and jug, and there was even a little chamber pot to match the set.

The dressing table was the most artistic piece of furniture in the room. That, and the matching chairs, were white with fine gold designs painted on them, the oval mirror beautifully set in the midst of tiny side cupboards.

There were a few dolls but somehow these never came alive like the Dolls' House did. They were just plaster figures poorly clad. It was as if the house reminded me more of some ghostly family who had lived there in the past — a mirror of Victorian life.

It was in later years when I brought out my Dolls' House again to appreciate it with an adult mind that I came to realise what a fascinating world is enclosed in these things. No wonder the habit of collecting them has caught on among adults, not children, and they have become precious and carefully preserved antiques, not just to look at but to use to step into that unperceived world like Alice when she stepped through the looking glass.

★ ★ ★

My home was a vicarage in the North Midlands during the first world war. It was a strangely sheltered environment in comparison to life in this modern age, almost bounded by the nursery window or at any rate the garden fence.

There were however other worlds both great and imaginary, which I must have heard my parents talk of and which captured my imagination. I was reminded of this by finding a tiny booklet I had meticulously made. It is only about 3 by 2 inches. The cover is ornamented by a detailed map I seem to have drawn of the area, giving some marvellous details.

It is written in pencil and a very childish hand and this is fast fading with age. I found it quite by accident among my papers in a drawer. On opening its faded pages made from scraps of a lined notebook with the lines running down instead of across, this is what I read.

ALL ABOUT ROSELAND.
Chapter I
The Counties. The Wilds.

If you wish to hear all about Roseland the best place to start from is the Wilds, or The Black Jungle as some call it because it is so dense and there are a number of wild animals in it.

There are a good many English ones such as the Lion Tiger Puma wild cat monkeys and a few bears.

How much I must have been a child of the British Empire period to label these animals as English. After all in those days India was under the Raj.

The book continues:

The picture on the next page shows a dragon mouse. These little animals build nests in the long grass of the wilds. They are most amusing little things and are often kept as pets.

The antler cat who is seen in our picture is a dangerous animal and has been known to kill men with its antlers.

A certain part of the wilds a little bit on the outskirts has been cut down and a small village with two or three shops and a post office and a couple of hotels and a few shooting boxes.

This is where the big game shooters stay when they are not staying out or at home.

The wilds are not all together [altogether is meant, presumably] the isolated tract we think as in a good part of it, there are little railways cut through it. The railway carriages are like a toy railway they are awfully small.

There are a lot of little platforms with a hut or two near it, dotted up and down the line. This is where the train stops.

This is when it drops and takes the mails from and to the camping parties who are shooting there.

We must now leave the wilds and travel to another point but I must say one more thing before we do so. There are two sorts of campers, there are the game shooters and also there are a sort of half black gipsy who if annoyed can be very dangerous. There are not many but sometimes you may meet a camp full of them.

We now travel on to Yarpoint. Almost an historic place because of the battle when Walter was King of Mersinbigum Island near.

Then the story of Roseland ends alas, although there is plenty of room for much more on this page 5, as the last page is numbered.

Who was Walter? Strange name for a king — and what was the island kingdom like that he ruled over?

What an odd story to write but on reflection typical of the world of those days as a child saw it. The English animals, lion, tiger, puma etc., all animals foreign to our country we should say today but in those days under the British Raj in India they seemed to the child as a British possession, part of Britain. Also in spite of a love of pet animals in the family, the big game shooter was a sort of hero. Shooting tigers was something King George always did when he went to India. You must shoot them, they were dangerous animals, was the slogan.

Brigadier Sleeman had not obliterated this myth then as he did later when he went through such a country *entirely without a gun* and carrying a camera instead which showed pictures of a family of lions eating breakfast amicably close to his camp having been provided with a haunch or two of meat slung from a tree by their thoughtful host.

There were no national parks in those days, no World Wildlife Organisation. How strange that the policy towards wild life has become less violent and yet the volume of violence has increased among mankind.

I think that the story of Roseland, since it is about what seemed to me as the real world, must have been intended as a real literary effort, although Roseland of course was a myth.

Then there was another type of kingdom that I created in my imagination and which I often spoke of but I cannot find anything written about. Perhaps I felt myself that it was all too mythical to set down in cold fact.

It was I suppose a kind of Utopia where everything happened just as you wanted it to happen; anything missing here was provided there, a valuable compensation for the frustrations of childhood. Chiefly I remember the sense of superiority it gave me to be able to say how things were done in this world of mine for it seemed almost as if I was ruler of it.

This kingdom went by the extraordinarily uninspired name of Jab Jab, hardly compatible with Roseland, and yet it was far more a bed of roses probably than one full of big gamehunters and warrior kings!

The reason for this sharp even belligerent sounding name was probably because my kingdom idea suffered some competition from my brother who immediately invented one, just to encourage me I expect, and he called his Boberyslob. I cannot think why, except that Nanny called him Bobbin. So he might have felt that Bob was suitable for the root of it and slob was rather a typical boyish sound of contempt. I can imagine how faced with this battle of words I would have replied in a sort of self-defence, Jab Jab!

Besides these imaginary kingdoms there were also individuals. I claimed a sort of exclusive friendship with 'My Lady'. She was a well known figure and I constantly referred to her. According to my mother and Nanny I recall feeling a certain amount of quiet prestige when I was able to tell them that My Lady says this or believes that. She was married and had two children, Stanley and a girl, whose name I can't recall.

Most surprising of all was the other invisible contact, Miss Dartchett. She seemed to have innumerable children and I could not make out why the grown ups smiled so when I mentioned this interesting fact. However I insisted this was so and felt I had said something rather important, since it caused such a reaction among grown ups.

I cannot recall at what age I dispensed with these fantasies. It would have been very interesting to know.

After this my literary efforts appear to have turned to more realistic matters in my own country. I put together with some stitching an exciting little periodical called *The Private Eye*. This was much larger than Roseland. It was about the size of a paperback. On the cover was the rather hideous profile of a girl, probably of school age, with her hair tied back tight and an enormous eye flanked by a rather inquisitive nose that looked as if it was smelling out things. But the eye was the important thing and out of all proportion to the rest of the face. Under the title was the explanation that this was a Private Detective periodical! It is a great pity that I can't find the original because I cannot quite recall what had been detected, or what we were to try to detect in the future.

It was a strange jump from the kingdom of Roseland and its admiration of the Empire, something my brother never shared; I think that he had probably taken an interest in boys' detective stories and I, since it was my great wish to imitate him, had decided to manufacture my own home-made brand.

What children were reading at that time is a matter of some interest. I came across recently an old letter written by my cousin Charlie, who had our beloved Nanny before she came to us. Nanny must have treasured it all these years. I include it here as it is enlightening in both literature and psychology for children in those days.

The letter begins with her nickname which probably came from her Christian name which was Agnes and he altered to Agpag. The letter is undated but it must have been written about 1905 which is when Nanny came to us and probably posted a book to her recent charge as a birthday present or something.

It shows that *Peter Pan* is just beginning to make an impact on the children of those days. He refers to it as 'a book of that name' not just as *Peter Pan*, concluding that everyone will know now what he means as anyone would later on.

The injunctions of Father to finish Nanny's

gift first, 'to stick to' it before he starts on the doubtless tempting book to become a children's classic, is typical of the ethic of that age. Unfortunately the pendulum has swung too far to the other extreme now.

Tadley,
Basingstoke.

My dear Agpag,
I hope you are very well. Thank you very much indeed for the book. It is very interesting. I like it very much. I am so sorry that you have been unfortunate with your teeth. I hope both your sisters are very well too. I have got another book called *Peter Pan*! But I am reading yours first, as Pater says that it is best to stick to one and read it through. I have also had a football, and a box of 'Turkish Delight' from Mrs Stroud. I use my bycicle a lot, it is very usfull. I have made up a story out of my own head and I am illustratting it; it is called 'The Adventures of a Mouse'. The mouse is called Bob-tail. We are not having very nice weather here it is rainy and windy.

Here the letter ends.
The children's annual, and one which

20

might influence our lives then, was the *Chatterbox*. It was rather indicative of the kind of attitude towards children that it was called by this name. 'Be quiet, you chatterbox' was the sort of term of friendly contempt used by grown-ups in those days for it seldom dawned on them that children had anything of importance to say as it does today. However I don't believe we ever stopped to think of that so thrilled were we to get hold of this book. Its characters were adopted by us immediately. Nanny played Joey the parrot, a name she was known by for many years after, and Ralph the fierce part of Tiger Tim which probably satisfied the growing aggressiveness of boyhood. Curiously enough, I can't recall what part I took. Perhaps I was only a looker on when Nanny and Ralph re-enacted these episodes together.

My natural milieu was much more in the confines of 'Little Folks'. I became very sympathetic regarding the homes for sick children, especially the convalescent home at Bexhill. I have never visited the town myself and so for me the childish image of the home still represents it in my mind, a place of concern and compassion still.

Perhaps the most potent reflection of the thoughts of those times comes in the scrapbooks that Nanny compiled for us, with her own hands. They were full of the cut outs of individual figures of children obviously from shop catalogues. The outstanding features of them are the innumerable layers of frills that characterised summer dresses or hats and the formal shape of garments, even those in the heavier tweeds. Clear-cut lapels and padded shoulders, shaped waists and outstanding skirts below them in imitation of the grown ups. How could small children relax comfortably and play in these formal clothes?

Now and then we glimpsed what was worn under them in models clad in heavy woollen knickers with legs long enough to include kneecaps. One model had a quilted kind of camisole with straps and appeared to be something in the nature of a new and exciting idea and was given a place of honour pasted on a picture of a garden of some stately home, which formed a strange background.

It was years before central heating was invented, or perhaps we should say revived as the Romans had it centuries ago. House insulation was unknown. As a Scandinavian Minister once said to me, 'An English house has sixty different kinds of draughts and I am generally sitting in one of them.' Poor man, he found it such an agony staying here in the war. Then also there were no antibiotics yet invented and pneumonia and even croup were very often killers among children. So perhaps the nannies of those days were justified in putting warm clothes to the fore.

Nanny's scrapbook started however with a pious picture entitled 'Oh day of rest and gladness' in colour showing an immaculately dressed Father in a frock coat leading a small girl in a smart red hat and coat and a boy in a sailor suit by the hand. They are walking up the path to the Church obviously followed by Mother and an Auntie, equally fashionably attired, while Grandpa with a neatly cropped white beard just appears over Mother's shoulder. The servants no doubt remained at home to cook the Sunday dinner. This was the picture of the ideal family in those days, when any backsliding was so discreetly hidden.

Nanny seems also to have had a great concern about drinking tea and there are innumerable pictures of this starting with an eighteenth-century picture of a gentleman in a velvet coat and knee breeches with buckle shoes and two ladies, one with a lace shawl and cap, presumably the wife, with a dutiful daughter with no cap and a low cut bosom pouring tea out of a lustre tea pot. A pure white cloth covers the table with a home-made cake that is tempting even today in the faded picture.

Then there is a little girl in a dress of pale pink chiffon with a swathed sash. Even she is burdened with a large pink hat and she is proffering a cup of tea in a blue tea cup with a matching teapot also on a white tea cloth, but to the modern mind perilously near the edge of the table, since anyone moving quickly might accidentally push it off.

Mixed up with this is a picture of George V as Prince of Wales in uniform and medals, as if to remind us that tea was a product of the Empire.

Further on we get another pious picture that brings back memories, entitled 'The Evening Hymn', Sing it with Mother. There is the little upright piano with the old brass candle sticks attached exactly as we had at the Vicarage. In the picture a little girl is sitting on her mother's knee while the latter taps out the notes. In our case, we used to gather round, my brother and I and my mother, and sing all the familiar hymns at this time like this.

Below this there is another tea drinking ceremony. A picture of a Darby and Joan.

She, with a knowing look, is lifting the lid of the teapot, he cupping his ear to listen as if tea could talk. There is no cake in the empty dish; perhaps they could not afford one but a white kitten with blue eyes adds ornament to the ceremony.

After that there are a lot of views of some grand surroundings, bushy gardens; it might be sections of Kew but the place is not specified. Then comes a glorious colour piece. Soldiers of all kinds including Sikhs in turbans and at the front Scottish men in kilts and Guardsmen in busbies, Australians, Canadians and a black servant, sitting on the ground, and then the caption:

One Queen, One Flag, One Empire.

After this patriotic utterance we go back to a lot more flowers and cosy children, pages of them, and then comes the end with a coloured picture of the Coronation of Edward VII, rays of gold descending on him from Heaven and other angles and also on to a cosy little church too and the surrounding land, the whole presided over by a strange sort of guardian angel in a steel helmet. How lucky people were in the security of that age but as if a shadow of things to come there is also a picture of an urbane gentleman, with a large tin labelled 'Kill It' under one arm, distributing it liberally through a watering can in his other hand as he walks along a flower bed. A new wonder? No, the beginning of the poisoned world we know today loaded with garden sprays like this but not so plainly labelled 'Kill It' today for fear people would be put off and would not buy it.

The second scrapbook of a later date is only done on brown paper. Children have taken a big step forward. They are shown in the series of pictures entitled 'Harrods Painting Competition', 'My birthday month', wearing reasonably short clothes without any frills and taking independent action, one on a tricycle and another in a toy motor advancing at such a pace as to scare the local geese away! Another boy is sitting in a strange hand-propelled machine while his friends wave him on with delight from a green hillside. Truly an age of action beginning, with independence and mechanical transport. Only the design for the month of December when it should be full of Christian love returns to the old ethics. The boy, attired in a boy scout's uniform, plus hat, and holding up a Union Jack in triumph, is standing on a prostrate Red Indian!

This movement towards action also came out in my brother's preoccupation with toy aeroplanes, *The Wonders of Aviation*, as the book that he acquired was entitled. In those days when Ian Dunne, author of *Experiment with Time*, was only just inventing the first aeroplane in which you could stand up, it was very easy to wonder at these comparatively normal achievements as we should think of them today. My mother became most anxious about these developments. She feared my brother would take up flying when he grew up and it was a dangerous life and he would be killed. It was not the aeroplane, but a motor bike that was to terminate his life here on earth some years later.

The Marvels of Modern Aviation was another book in my brother's collection. I still have it. Even the first pages which consist of advertisements for other books are a revelation regarding the attitude to life and its discoveries in those days. The Library of Romance covers two pages, each title beginning with the words *The Romance of* — . There is the *Romance of Savage Life* describing the adventures and sports of primitive man. There is even *The Romance of Modern Sieges* though these are hardly a military operation in which one could think much romance could be found. Incredibly, it is written by a clergyman. There is also *The Romance of Mining*. That was before the days of the Gresford disaster, of course, and after the elimination of child labour from the mines. There was a library of heroes too. *Heroes of Missionary Enterprise* and *Heroines of Missionary Adventure.* We are told these record true stories of Intrepid Bravery, stirring adventure with uncivilised man and wild beasts.

This seems strangely different to the utterances of people like Bishop Huddlestone who suggests today that we can only go to Africa and sit in a native style hut in the forest and hope people will come to us after what we have done. Wild beasts and struggles against them are hardly in line with the world-wide movement for the preservation of world wild life. Perhaps we have progressed in some ways nearer the truth but at the expense of an aura of romance that cloaked reality with a rosy hue.

Another in the Hero series was described as true stories of intrepid bravery and stirring adventures of the pioneers, Explorers and Founders of Modern Africa.

A newspaper's comment on it is that 'A more stirring and instructive book for lads than this would be hard to find.' Yet there appears to be no thought for the people from whom the present day rulers of modern Africa are drawn, the Africans themselves who really owned the land from time immemorial.

The book itself is in the early part devoted to ballooning and gliding as early forms of locomotion in the air but it moves on to flying later and observes, 'Every man who first entrusts his life to the supporting power of the invisible air whether in a parachute or an aeroplane feels the thrill of adventure the romance of the unknown tingling in his blood!'

Does this attitude characterise the sophisticated crowds who step on and off the enormous jets capable of carrying 300 people and which, bar sabotage, make the journey safely across the world? Have we by very necessity become so acclimatised to the unexpected including accidents that we take quite calmly the loss of several hundred lives in an air liner?

The drama of early accidents is recorded in my brother's book thus:

Perhaps the first serious accident was that in which Captain Dickson and Thomas were involved in Milan in October 1910. Dickson was flying on his Farman Biplane at a comparatively low altitude. Thomas was far above him on an Antoinette Monoplane. The Monoplanist could not see immediately beneath him and the biplanist's upward vision was obscured by the upward plane. Thomas began to descend and the spectators realised that a collision was possible. They shouted to both the aviators warnings, but naturally their cries were not heard in the machines. Swiftly the monoplane swooped down like a gigantic eagle dropping on its prey. Then occurred a catastrophe that realised all that the most vivid imagination had ever conjured up concerning aerial collisions. The undercarriage of the monoplane crashed through the up plane of Dickson's machine and the two planes dropped to earth locked in inextricable confusion. Dickson sustained terrible injuries including a fractured pelvis and for a fortnight was delirious, yet he was restored by the arts of the physician to something like his health and strength. Thomas was unhurt.

The catastrophe that 'realised all that the most vivid imagination had ever conjured up' seems small in comparison to the terrible and gigantic accidents that occur today. Airplanes that are now looked on when overhead as something of a modern pest and the proposal of a new aerodrome a source of gigantic opposition and demonstration in those days were as rare as an endangered species.

I have been recently looking at my brother's letters written home from his prep school. After he has got off his mind the ever occurring anxiety had he gone up or down in his place in the form for the week — and how this fact seemed to dominate his life in spite of my parents' tolerance about it — aeroplanes were of next importance in the news.

We had an aeroplane over on Wednesday morning. I think it was Wednesday just before the bell. It was very low but I did not see it as I had gone into the next room that does not have a window, that way I only heard it. I also saw one on Thursday and it was going in your direction.

He writes as if the event was remarkable. As if his thoughts are on things in high spheres he adds, 'That Comet I wrote to you about can now be seen through a telescope, you had better watch out for it.' And ending with the more mundane but joyous statement, 'Daddy is coming a fortnight next Saturday.'

Why he was coming without Mummy I cannot think and as his mother must know this fact it would seem that it was joyous anticipation made him write it, and fear

31

that if he does not state it the fact might be forgotten and the hope fade. It is rather like a prisoner anticipating the next visit and why should it have to happen to a boy with a good home. He was always saying to my mother, 'Can't you have me home and have me privately tortured?' Why should he be sent away at seven years old?

A further letter returns to the excitement of the second plane by stating;

That aeroplane was a biplane after all. I only saw it far away and could not tell, a boy told me it was a triplane but I have learnt since it was wrong.

The aviator was going to land on Stafford Common Some children were in his way. They ran to meet it. Tried to rise. Could not. Biff! Machine ruined. Aviator bruised. No-one else hurt.

Strangely uninformed of those children. They ran to meet this strange creature. They knew nothing of self-preservation in the path of such vehicles, since there were no visits to aerodromes then!

As aeroplanes became such a dominant interest my brother, in company with many other boys of his time, acquired several model ones. These were made of light frames

32

with a transparent sort of oilskin stretched over them for wings. There was a propeller activated by a long piece of elastic which you wound round and round. Then you flung it into the air and the propeller kept revolving until the elastic was unwound. The flight of such a plane and its progress was a matter of great importance to my brother; in fact we all stood and watched it go in amazement.

It was indeed an age of locomotion as was portrayed in our scrapbook, for when my brother was not launching things into the air he was riding about speedily on his bicycle. This was something in which I could join. I acquired a bicycle too and after some awful adventures when my brother, used to the more spartan environment of his prep school, launched me off on it in rather the casual manner that he did his model aeroplanes and with the same detached curiosity as to where I would end up, I finally mastered the secret of balance and found I could go alone on it.

It seems extraordinary that one could wobble off on the road from our village almost to the next, a matter of a mile or two, only able to stop when you came to a hill and fell off, and never meet anything on the road to collide with. Somehow it never entered one's head that you might do. The road as far as we were concerned was ours, for our sole use.

When we moved to the smaller vicarage on what was, as Daddy said so appropriately, called 'The Rocks' I had a great opportunity to impose my skill on a bicycle. The garden and surroundings were not so big, now. An active occupation we could both participate in was bicycling round and round the outside of the house. This like a car rally caused one to encounter all sorts of terrain on the route. There was the gravel path at the front of the house, the jutting flowerbeds to be circumnavigated and the pear tree to miss, which stood against the house wall. But most exciting of all was when you rose over a ridge of blue bricks marking the entry and, narrowly missing the water butt, entered the yard. As my brother was riding at top speed in the other direction it took quite a lot of skill to avoid a collision and there were several near shaves when we met in either gateway to the yard.

It was I think this developed skill in manoeuvring and being quick to see, even prepared to see, your way almost blocked when you rounded a corner that stood me in such good stead later when I learnt to drive a car. I can recommend it as a good start.

There were however other activities that I

developed on my own, especially gardening. The house being too small for us my parents put a shed up at the edge of the kitchen garden at the side of the house. It was somewhat erroneously called 'The Nursery'. I don't know why because we had got past that stage, but the playroom would not have been part of our familiar vocabulary. All the toys were kept there but the thing that mattered to me most was that I was given the land just outside the nursery window for my very own garden. It contained a large border and a path up to the other border under the hedge. In front the border was full of tall flowers like lupins and delphiniums. This was intersected by a circle of grass in the middle of which stood a wooden post, with an old sundial placed on it. This seemed to me the focus of the garden, with the soft turf leading up to it and the velvet pansies in the border round it. It was somehow linked with those romantic pictures of a garden that occurred in the Dolls' House pictures and others I had seen.

The glorious colour of the tall plants, pink and blue lupins and the deeper blue of the delphiniums, used to look lovely on a fine summer day. This was my own domain.

I took it all, very seriously, buying gardening papers and devouring them hungrily.

In those days things seemed so much more simple; you bought a plant or a packet of seeds, put them in and they grew. No complicated fertilisers. Periodically some farmer would put a load of horse manure at the garden gate, to be hastily got in and distributed over all areas. I recall one awful episode when it came late and our gardener could not come that afternoon to put it in, and a neighbour coming by in the dark fell on top of it! We had to apologise profoundly afterwards. How lucky we were that a car did not go into it, but now I come to think of it so few people owned cars, not anyone up our little lane except ourselves.

We were lucky in having a splendid gardener. His name was Ben Sedgewick but for some reason that I can't recall he was always known as Potter Boo. He was not of course a full time one. He had a responsible job at the pit letting the cage up and down the pit. He was called a Winder. But he came to us when his shift at the pit allowed him time during daylight to do the garden and somehow it fitted in well.

He had his own views about gardening and would always fill the borders round the front of the house inevitably with red geraniums and yellow calceolarias and blue lobelia at the front. Sometimes we longed for a little change but dared not suggest it. I do remember first meeting Siberian wallflowers in that area, so I suppose wallflowers mingled with them too.

There was only once that we really came into conflict. When being asked to put some unwanted turf at the back of the side border in my garden to form a useful windbreak he rushed it over there with all his strength and energy when I was not there and plonked it down on what I knew were the roots of my beloved Madonna lilies.

The great wall he built was far too heavy for me to move and I recall that the peaceful atmosphere of my garden was disturbed by my anger and frustration. But we solved the problem somehow!

Potter Boo will always be remembered for his philosophical phrase, 'See 'ow we go on!'

On the whole I found gardening a very peaceful occupation and foil to the locomotion activities which dominated our childhood.

2

Nanny Moves from the Lawn

One of the most beloved members of our household had been Nanny who came to us soon after my brother (who was five years older than me) was born. She had therefore been in our family for some years, when the mounting cost of prices caused by the war forced us to give her up. She was needed at home to look after her ageing mother so she remained there like a dutiful daughter.

When Nanny's mother died at last after a long illness we did our best to persuade Nanny to come back to us. I have letters from my brother and me condoling with her and begging her to do this. 'It would be so wonderful to have you again,' we say, showing how much we thought of her as a person. But it was not to be. Nanny was a Shropshire lass, the daughter of the village carpenter. She never really belonged to our colder climes of North Staffordshire and the mining community who really made up most of the parish when you got away from the select 'Church End'. We always teased her about her disgust when arriving at Treffdyn Terrace, Aberdovey, for our first seaside holiday, she was horrified to see a whole line of coal trucks labelled 'Foxfield Colliery' pass by in front of the windows along the Old Cambrian Line that ran between the houses and the sea. The Foxfield Colliery was the one actually in our parish down at Godley Brook and the strange smell of the bank on fire would permeate the vicarage even if you could not see the colliery from there.

Nanny elected to move from 'The Lawn' as her Shropshire home was known, down a steep hill nearer the village and live on the farm her sister and brother-in-law occupied with their two children, Myrtle and Hazel. Hazel, being the baby, was the object of her special concern and I felt rather symbolized in her mind the many babies she had cared for.

It was through her concern for Hazel that I first learnt of the power of bossy school mistresses through one who forbade Nanny even to enter the playground, for instance, when she took Hazel to school. No wonder there was a need for parent power. She would not get away with that nowadays with Parent Committees and their involvement in school matters which is encouraged today by the modern staff.

Then there was the problem of leaving that village school and the riding all round the countryside 'on one of those nasty buses' as Nanny described it, just when Hazel who was a nervous child was getting settled down.

I little knew then how modern communications would destroy the small village school altogether in many cases, although for the older ones it would make possible fields of higher education which were to be of great value to them.

When the two children were older their mother, Edie, began to take in paying guests in this large farm house romantically called The Grange. Nanny brought her furniture down from The Lawn including a beautifully made sideboard her father had done with a craftsman's hand and the long cupboard that stood in the sitting room at Hurst Cottage (before she moved to The Lawn). It was on these doors she used to measure my increased height each time I went to stay with her.

My Auntie Aggie's furniture cropped up there also because she went to stay there for a time and somehow arranged to leave it behind her.

There was her chair-bed, a fore runner of the put-you-up, I suppose, or modern divan. It did not seem to make into a chair at all but it had a decorative wooden rail round it forming the back and arms. This looked very nice but it was rather inconvenient when you were a tall person because as far as I can recall it did not let down either end to allow for your height when you got into bed. If it was still with us it would no doubt be very much revered today as an antique and fetch a lot at Christies. There was the upright piano too and a cupboard full of lots of pieces of china; in fact there were many charming knick-knacks in the way of ornaments all over the room and on the old-fashioned mantelpiece; that is what made it so fascinating. It was a large sized room, long in shape with a French window that looked out on to grass and a flower border. There was a wonderful show of lupins there if you went at the right time of year, of which Edie was very proud. In fact it was rather like Ruth Draper showing her garden and saying, 'You should have been here last week.'

So many people came and went there finding pleasure in a holiday in such beautiful country. Nanny often regaled us with accounts of them and the family stories which she knew well. They made almost novelettes in themselves. Most of the families came from the blacker parts of South Staffordshire, so the country was a real luxury to them. Nanny seemed to get to know them all and became personally concerned about their fortunes and misfortunes that beset them over the years afterwards.

There was a policeman used to come with his family quite frequently. He appears to have overlapped with a Norwegian boy I sent. As a result of this I got an excited letter from Nanny saying, 'Oh, dearest, has the right boy been chosen at last? The Norwegian boy said to policeman that he was going to marry an English lady called Miss P in two years' time!'

To which I could only reply I wish he would have told me this before he went to the police about it! I am afraid Nanny was disappointed because I did not feel that he was the right boy though he was a good friend of mine like so many Norwegians.

The most interesting would-be lodger that Nanny nearly had to gossip about at The Grange was the daughter of some old friends and next door neighbours at Daddy's old home.

I came across 'the letter' she had evidently sent to Nanny or her sister and I put it in this book verbatim because it is couched in such fascinating terms. It can hardly be called a letter since it is regailed almost as a story about herself and her problems and yet in a formal way that might better suit Royalty.

It is written on faded notepaper with a deep edge of black although she must have suffered the loss of her famous mother, with whom she lived, some time, even years, before this was written, judging by her account of the previous places she seems to have inhabited on her own.

Her mother was the daughter of a famous Victorian general. She wrote some very interesting books under a man's name about psychic phenomena which chiefly occurred at their home next door to my father's and which had belonged originally to a nearby Abbey and so had ancient foundations. But that is another story.

The document, if you can call it that, recounts the sad predicaments of unmarried ladies of that generation for whom no proper provision has been made when they relinquish the role of devoted daughter at home and, quite unsuited for any job, are forced to face the economic realities of life. The document begins:

April 19/42

at Vicarage
Nr Stafford

Miss G. is trying to find a bed sitting-room for herself.

43

She believes she is writing to people in whose house Miss Aggie Plant and Mrs George Plant used to stay, she wonders if they remember Miss Aggie Plant speaking of her. The families were very dear friends —

Miss G. has been lodging at a Vicarage for 6 months — Here she has had 2 rooms and done her own cooking and house-work, but it is too expensive for her here, and she thought perhaps in a very quiet country place it might be easier — if boarding it might not really be very expensive and perhaps not easy to do for herself — she likes to but it might not be allowed.

She is 65 and strong and well except for about a month she has suffered from rheumatism, but this is rather a damp place.

She thinks she remembers that a Curate used to lodge at Blymhill Grange, and thinking that the old Vicar might be dead, and no Curate needed, the lodgings might be to let?

Her difficulty is this — she has from her home at the Old Vicarage some very much prized furniture enough for one room — She cant sell it as she has only a Life Interest in it — also she has to

44

keep books and papers belonging to her Mother.

She has: 1 Bureau; a small sea-chest; a very nice oak chest; a book case; 4 small bookcases; a good many books, photographs and pictures, a long carpet rug arm-chair, small arm-chair small rocking chair 1 chair she bought in coming here — rocking-chair 2 other chairs — A screen. A little piece of oil.

When she was at the local Convent all this went into 1 room not large and there was bed, wash stand 2 wardrobes belonging to convent in as well.

Since coming to lodge here, Miss G.K. has set herself up with enough things to manage with independently of the vicarage — sheets, crockery, a bed and meat safe, but need not bring the bed if no room for it and the lodgings would rather theirs was used

She has blankets and a little silver — Mrs George Plant knows Miss G.K. if there is need to write to anyone. She is Church of England. She thinks she is not at all difficult to live with but likes to be quiet in the country. Please say if Miss G.K. shd come over to look at rooms also what the terms wd be — if house-kept for or if living in and looking after herself.

Please answer soon she is writing to several places. She has black out curtains.

Could you tell her of any nice place if not able to have her and if you are Miss Plants.

It is a pity that the letter from Miss G.K. ends there, perhaps the other page has been lost down the years. It would have been so interesting to learn how she ended it. Was it in words comparable to its strangely formal style rather akin to a running commentary, or did she at the end lapse into something a little more personal like 'yours sincerely' for instance. I'm amazed when people even slightly below a Cabinet Minister are called by their Christian names by radio interviewers. There seems a strange contrast between that and the formal and distant approach made in this letter.

Actually nothing came of it. Perhaps it was not any cheaper than the vicarage, or it proved impossible to take in all the furniture, or the curate in question was still in residence?

The curate was another of the interesting paying guests that Nanny had to look after. The vicar of the parish was, as so often happened in those days, the younger brother of the earl at the big house. This filled to a great extent the niche required of him when family and prestige were strongly mingled with things pertaining to God, just like the Empire was. He lent dignity and importance to the church and although he was rather a remote figure, he satisfied the county folk, I think quite well.

The curate was also high in the social hierarchy having a titled mother but had rather a different type of churchmanship. He was an ardent Anglo-Catholic, and also developed a close link of friendship with members of the orthodox church and the Balkans. It was said that one day a man appeared who did not speak a word of English but had found his way all the way from Yugoslavia, merely murmuring the priest's name.

Nanny who had been used to plain C of E was not very versed in these 'goings on' especially when they involved her in providing special food for certain days. Abstinence before a Saint's Day was a mystery to her and she invariably served up something excessively liberal like meat on a day that should have been a fast as she confided to us.

After that it became a family joke and if we gave her a frock that seemed rather good, my mother would laugh and say, 'Now, Nanny, don't forget, *don't* wear it on Vigil days!'

The curate finally entered an Anglican order where the practice of such pious observances was all a matter of daily life. He became so caught up in higher consciousness however, that on one occasion he overlooked a staircase at the monastery altogether and fell right down it. His mother being a forthright and important titled lady, came straight over to the monastery on hearing the news and breached all the rules by striding up to his bedroom, a part of the building where women were strictly forbidden normally! However, her son, and his fellow monks recovered from their shock at this and I am glad to say he lived happily to a ripe old age in the safety of the order he had chosen.

This problem of getting the person into the right niche where they can flourish is rather like removing a plant from its pot and putting it in the right ground.

When Nanny's brother-in-law died and they were bound to move from The Grange, they first of all took a little house on the outskirts of a nearby town, one of a whole group all close together. They were comparatively recently built with most modern conveniences but the family never felt settled there although there must have been much less to do or worry about than at the old farm. Then after a time they heard of what the agents would call 'a cottage of character' but as yet in some places the value of such things had not been realised by the rich townsmen moving out. The price was well in their reach and they secured it. A lovely old cottage outside the town standing a little away from neighbours with a nice strip of garden in which they could grow their own vegetables, and a place for a run full of lusty hens.

The long low hedge bordered the main road down which there was a constant stream of traffic — only one lorry, however, diverted from its normal path got stuck in the hedge!

Otherwise everything went sailing by and Nanny and Edie in their big coats and hats were distinctive figures peeping over the hedge at the coach to Liverpool and the long distance lorries, quite invigorated and content to be interested spectators and watch the world go by.

3

Leisure Activities

An important event in the life of our village at home was the whist drive. In those days no one had television as a window on the world, nor in the earlier days even wireless. So that these communal events were absolutely essential outlets. They were generally in aid of something, but that was really a minor matter, an excuse for holding them.

Everybody got very busy beforehand planning all the arrangements. First there were the prizes to be got together mostly through people's generosity, Ladies' first prize, Gentlemen's first prize and even a Consolation Prize or Booby Prize for those who did not do so well.

Then there was the food much of which was home-made and provided by the ladies of the committee. The whist drive was followed by a dance that went on till 2 a.m. so the supply of food had to be extensive to last the night.

These events were held in the uninspiring precincts of the village school but this did not seem to damp the energy and enthusiasm of the helpers. The Endowed School it was called but what it was endowed with, I am not sure — perhaps it was only with necessities before state education came in. It was not a nice little cosy place like the small village school in more rural parts of the country. It was a tall rather bleak building surrounded by hard concrete yards. It was built at the far end of the village near to the colliery and my memory of it is mostly on winter nights when a biting cold wind seemed to sweep round the angles of the building and through those barren concrete playgrounds where there was not the slightest escape from it.

Once the whist drive had started silence reigned because the game was taken very seriously indeed. How far the wish to obtain a prize entered into it is hard to tell. Prowess at the game was an important factor. Most people had played whist all their lives and welcomed the opportunity to use their skill. There were well-known adepts at it and anyone who got them as a partner was considered lucky.

It never struck me at the time how the class division that was so apparent in those days was demonstrated even in the world of cards. The village played whist but all

51

our friends played bridge. There were lots of bridge parties in the afternoon social occasions for the womenfolk before they had to get home to welcome their husbands back from their jobs.

Whist was a good stimulant to the brain and concentration for those who took part in the drives probably better than the more formal social events of bridge parties where people often went to show off their frocks as much as their mental capacity.

The dance was a lively affair in spite of the energy which had been put into whist by the older generation. Now it was the young people's turn, and they added very much to the gaiety of the dance, which was by no means a clod-hopping affair as a whole. The population were very sensitive to music and this made them ready to respond to the rhythms of the dance and display a high standard.

Of course it was the subject of constant gossip who danced with whom and surmise as to the permanence of their future relationships. It must have been very difficult to sample the different young people in a group for even one dance would set tongues wagging, let alone two dances.

These events were long sessions and meant leaving the house empty for we had no servants after the first world war. We could not afford them. There was no central heating so fires had to be stacked up with slack and a good guard put across them.

On one occasion fearing it might go out my father hit on the splendid plan of sending a parishioner to make it up again. He was a strange-looking little man, very shabby in his clothes rather resembling a tramp, of which we had many in those days.

After this was all arranged and the man had gone on the errand armed with our key to let himself in, my father suddenly remembered that the house was full of our pet beagles. What would they make of him when he came in! Would they sense an intruder and team up against him, suddenly reacting to the collective impulse that moves the pack sometimes. He began to remember a terrible story of a huntsman who went down in the night to a kennel of foxhounds because he heard a noise, clad only in his night shirt, not his normal huntsman's clothes, and in the morning only his boots were found.

However, much to his relief the parishioner came back beaming at his reception. The beagles had recognised him as a friendly visitor and got up and kissed him as they did everyone who came to the vicarage. Luckily beagles are not in the least class-conscious, they do not judge people's merit by their clothes, so his shabby appearance did not upset them. They recognised a real friend.

When the whist drive and dance were over and things cleared up it was after 2 a.m. Few people had cars in those days, most of them would collect in family parties with a good big lantern and trudge home though it might be quite a long walk. In fact there were a few tragic episodes resulted from this. Someone with flu just beginning would turn out from the warm crowded school to face the penetrating wind we were subject to in those parts and the result would be pneumonia. In those days such an illness could be a killer. There was no panel. Medical treatment had to be paid for and young mothers for this reason often sent for the doctor too late, because they feared they could not pay the bill, and death resulted leaving a motherless family.

Of course there were other activities, at times other than in winter. The Sunday School Treat, for instance, or the Prizegiving. It was amazing how attendances went up when any form of remuneration came near. You could not blame them when treats were so few and far between and books beyond their financial level. Everyone seemed to get a prize for something.

The Sunday School treat was an exciting affair because it meant a drive in a specially hired coach, which was a rare treat in itself. It was quite a business getting them all on to the coach plus the fat lady helpers and the mums who had asked to come to look after the much younger ones. But finally all were on board and rather like a coop of clucking chickens the vehicle moved off to its objective.

I seem to remember chiefly going to see the gardens of a famous house, Trentham Hall, which belonged to the Duke of Sutherland. In those days the family still lived in the house at times. I can't recall very much that was entertaining for the children other than a good tea, which was probably something of a luxury for them. In those days even glimpsing the seat of a duke was an awe-inspiring experience since there was no National Trust and the stately homes of England were seldom open to the public.

I chiefly recall walking by the river, the Trent, and my parents laughing about my grandmother's alarm when she heard it had become contaminated and she feared that it was near to us and might do us harm. It looked very stagnant as we walked along it in the grounds and I made a mental note that it was something to keep away from. This was, I think, my first memory of the contamination of the environment that was to play such a big part in community problems later on.

There were of course more lengthy outings connected with the adults in the village, the most important one being the Choir Trip on which we ventured much further afield but that deserves a separate chapter.

★ ★ ★

It was one of the drawbacks of the social conventions those days that one did not play with the village children. Even my democratic mother who had given up servants owing to financial pressures and rather prided herself on being a pioneer in 'scrubbing her own doorstep' as she described it did not think that I should play with the village children in the road.

I recall sallying forth with my pedal motorcar which caused considerable excitement as a rarity and was an object of envy among the local children. A little boy called George was particularly enamoured of it and although my mother called me back he decided evidently not to lose contact with us. At this time we had moved into a much smaller house and it was very easy to push open the door in the thick privet hedge and advance up the little path to the front door for a curious child. My mother, fearing we might be followed, drew me into the hall as it had no windows, thinking George seeing the rooms empty would conclude we were out and go away. Imagine our surprise when we heard the flap of the letter box rattle and we saw a pair of wonderful brown eyes peering at us through it. He had tracked us down.

It seemed a pity that social convention should cause me to have such a lonely childhood, since the social factor also caused my brother to go away to a prep school young and so I only had him in the holidays. But these factors did make me very much thrown back on my environment and to note every little detail of things I might not otherwise have had time to observe and take in.

Later on tennis became a popular game among people who had never thought of engaging in it before. The press was full of news about those early Wimbledon stars. There was the astounding Madame Suzanne Lenglen. My mother kept a photo of her from *The Tatler* leaping sky high in the air in pursuit of the ball, but after my mother had shown it to quite a lot of friends she suddenly realised that the photo revealed the fact that Madame Lenglen's short skirt did not cover her stocking tops and there was a gap revealing an area of bare leg which was not considered nice so she put it away hastily.

The social gap was very much bridged by the start of the village tennis club. Some neighbours who had a big house and land which they farmed had little time for the social activities of tennis. So they let their tennis lawn out to the village. It was at the top end of their garden and conveniently approached by a cart track at the side of the field, so the members who used it did not disturb the family absorbed with the farm work.

A lot of our friends among the village folk joined the schoolmaster's daughters in the choir and the young people from the farms nearby.

I recall one whom we nick-named in the family The Wang Bird because she addressed the ball with such ferocity and you heard the racquet whang as it sped away, whether it was with good effect or not I cannot recall, as her style of hitting it was the all-absorbing factor. She was dark with rather plain hair and severe features and tight clothes, which were the object of some criticism from the village folk, but she charmed some men, or dominated them, for she made a successful marriage ultimately and left the village.

Perhaps her forthright nature was due to her mother, a very tall lady with white hair taken back severely off her face with rather piercing blue eyes. She is immortalised in my mind for the practical term she used on many occasions: 'A little help is worth a deal of pity.' How true she was in her sentiment.

4

The Great Exhibition

Stoke-on-Trent station was never a romantic place in the early hours of the morning, although no other stations can have to their credit the fact that a peer proposed there (in the waiting room in the blackout) and was accepted and it proved a happy marriage.

When we foregathered there at 2 a.m., a somewhat hilarious party consisting of my parents and the village choir and a few old friends or hangers-on, even we felt a little chilled though we did not have a blackout to contend with then.

The choir outing was a regular thing of course but we had never before ventured so far away as London, and this was a special event — to see the Great Exhibition at Wembley. We had once been to Liverpool, another fairly large metropolis it seemed to us, and there had been some moments of crisis. There was that one for instance when we went over a Cunard liner. Before flying became an every day mode of travel a ship was an object of great interest, and some reverence. We toured it therefore in a sort of joyous anticipation looking at every detail. There was, however, one literally dark moment when we were passing down a corridor and the light seemed strangely obscured. My father suddenly became aware that this was because of a strange object stuffed into the main port hole. He pulled at it and suddenly realised to his alarm that it was the trousers of a choirboy, and the owner was inside them. Curiosity having overcome the boy he had decided that he wanted to get a view of the ship's surroundings from a vantage point and being a landlubber from the Midlands, never thought of going up on deck to see the view.

It was indeed lucky that my father checked the impulse by dragging him back or we should have had to send up that alarming cry 'Man overboard'.

I do not recall any moment of crisis on the train going to Wembley. I think we dozed mostly at that early hour because in those days steam trains were rather slow and it took some time to get there. We had most of us left home at midnight. It was not surprising that when we arrived at Wembley at the Great Exhibition I was in a sort of daze; it was so vast and so dazzling that it seemed more like a dream than real life.

Those were the days when Britain had a vast empire. You could wander from stand to stand seeing exhibitions portraying it. Scenery in selected views were displayed by each country. Food and native arts all were before you.

Strangely enough I remember best the stand where we could drink marvellous fruit juices and we seemed to go back and back there for more. As far as I can recall this was all part of the Australian stand but specially linked with Tasmania, and the drink I had was orange juice.

In fact food seems to have been linked tremendously with the place in my memories of it for my father was looking forward to eating curried prawns in one of the many restaurants when we chose to dine. There had been a big sensation because a dentist from Wembley had eaten them and died from the effects. My father being an optimistic easy-going person laughed at the idea that he should suffer the same fate. Hundreds of people, he argued, must have eaten them and not died from food-poisoning. But my mother was a much more anxious person and it became a point of considerable argument between them. However in the end so far as I can recall he had them and survived.

Every time I go into London by train I

pass that building that housed the Great Exhibition. It is just part of the familiar landscape now. It certainly is very high but one no longer regards it with the veneration that we did then. I have since been to many events there so it has become familiar; also in these days everything is larger and I suppose we have rather altered our idea of normal dimensions.

The choir had to return home after this dazzling experience, they must have been very tired, but we were lucky we had arranged to stay with my father's sister and her husband at their little house in the Golders Green Garden suburb, so we could go home to an early bed.

A fascinating new world opened for us now. Coming from a village like ours, parts of which were disfigured by the back to back cottages, all that was provided for the miners, and knowing the grime and cost of life at the pit all these cosy little houses nestling in hedges and lovely gardens all somewhat resembling each other, but individual, fascinated me. I thought that something had been achieved in urban homes without destroying too much.

I was not to know how the development of the Golders Green area was the cause of such regret to some people who recalled its now incredible rural character which its name portrays.

I came across an old letter from an artist friend we had met while staying at an hotel in Surrey, a painter of flowers, she gave us as a present a most glorious water colour of red Iceland poppies in a blue vase, which, alas, much to my regret was lost in a fire at my house.

The letter starts off with a compliment to my mother with which she was so very pleased that I have always preserved the whole.

Thorlands Hotel,
Haslemere,
Surrey.

6 March 1927.

Dear Beautiful Mrs Plant,

I was so disappointed on returning yesterday to find that you had already left. I shall never meet anyone so statuesque again.

On Friday I went to see Miss Gerard and Miss Clarke, they admire you just as much as I do, and so would any discerning and appreciative person. They are living for a few weeks in their flat at Golders Green. Have you seen that part lately? It is, to me, simply amazing. The last time I was there, and not long ago, it was just fields with dusty hedges and I remember a man at one corner had rigged up 'Aunt Sallies' to divert the passer-by, if he should have a few minutes to spare.

But now it is a magnificent tho'fare, a wide handsome road, with big stylish shops on both sides. That is North End Road, which was just a little country lane, so lately. The house we used to visit was the Manor House, North End Road — and it was the only house on that side of the road, with extensive grounds of its own.

Our friends there, to be sure, died of old age, the grounds have become a town, and the Manor House itself is turned into a hospital.

Sic transit gloria mundi. 'The boast of heraldry, the pomp of power, and all that beauty, all that life can give await alike the inevitable hour' etc.

The second page with the signature was apparently lost. Her name was Bertha Macguire.

Auntie Mamie was one of Daddy's many sisters but she was especially linked with us because it was she who had supplied us with that wonderful person, Nanny. She came to us after she had been Nanny to Little

Charlie, as their son was called in order to distinguish him from his father. Ironically he became so tall when he grew up that he came to be known as Lofty.

I come to realise now that no one ever asked how they found Nanny in the first place, since Uncle Charlie was a curate in the Potteries when Aunt Mamie married him and they moved after that to Denton near Manchester. Nanny lived away on the Staffordshire-Shropshire borders. There were no job centres in those days and people did not advertise much in papers. How did they find this pearl of great price, my Nanny, who was to have such an impact on my life?

Uncle Charlie's father was vicar of Tadley in a corner of Berkshire and Hampshire and Nanny used often to describe walks round Tadley Gorse and the gypsies who lived there. She little knew then that the fields surrounding it would become one great housing estate for the staff at the huge nuclear plant at Aldermaston and that a flat normal-looking field by the pub would become famous as the Falcon Field where a canon of St Paul's Cathedral and other famous men would declaim the horrors and dangers of a new discovery, the atom bomb. How far removed it seemed from the quiet of life at a rural country vicarage then.

However Uncle Charlie seems to have somewhat disturbed the cultural peace by running a magazine among friends with some very avant-garde articles in it.

That he was a very sincere man was shown in a story Nanny told about the explosion at the hat factory at Denton which took place when they lived there and in which some employees died. When he discovered that it had been due to using an inflammable dye for the hats he was so upset that as a protest he never wore a hat again.

He became more and more impatient about all the poverty he saw around him, and the complacency of many people about it and finally resigned from the priesthood. For a time they went to Germany after this for him to fill a post as school master. They also became vegetarians. It was ironical that when they returned to England the only work he could obtain was as a clerk in the Smithfield Meat Market.

In the Garden Suburb of those days they found many friends with things in common especially in Fabian circles. That Aunt Mamie had something of the literary urge in her also, is indicated by the wife of the writer Horace Shipp (who in later years came to live beside us in Buckinghamshire). She related how Aunt Mamie had asked her

67

if she could possibly find her a quiet room in which to write a book. I don't think the idea ever materialised, however.

We stayed with them on several occasions after this but I don't recall that we ever discussed their views. Perhaps it was a good thing because I recall that we were in those days so narrow-minded as to express horror when we heard that they had actually shaken hands with Bernard Shaw! His sharp and amusing criticisms of the establishment pierced our cosy psychology too much.

Later Uncle Charlie became a Communist; again he never spoke of his faith but my most vivid memory of him is sitting in his chair beside a small book case on which was a bust of Trotsky. He sat with a board on his knee rolling with sensitive fingers the cigarettes made only from tobacco grown in his garden, so keen was he, I suppose, not to patronise the large capitalist firms.

In appearance he was a gentle blue-eyed man with a short red beard; a biblical picture more like my idea of one of the disciples than a Communist, I found it very puzzling to understand this.

I don't recall much of the sight-seeing we did in London, except the Tower of London where I turned sick and faint, probably owing to the horrible instruments of torture they showed us and the stories of all those who had died on the scaffold there.

What I recall most is bowling along in an old-fashioned red bus, usually sitting on the open top holding on to one's hat in the resulting wind and almost on the shores of the Welsh Harp. Not being used to great cities that open space and huge area of water and the fierce breezes off it were nectar to me.

The aunt and uncle were very kind to us. Aunt Mamie had a lovely sense of humour like Daddy and a sort of childish impulsiveness. I shall never forget my alarm when walking up Hoop Lane from the main road we passed the famous Golders Green Crematorium and Daddy said quite suddenly, 'I say let's go inside and see what happens!'

Off he and Auntie Mamie went, inviting Mummy and me to follow but she saw how upset I was at the thought. So she stayed with me outside. After some time Daddy and Auntie Mamie came out looking very pleased with themselves and saying, 'I say you should have come. It was awfully interesting!' It gave me a horror of crematoriums for years after that.

Rather luckily, however, Uncle Charles elected to move from Golders Green and the vicinity of the Crematorium to the more humble part of Harrow on a newly built estate. Whether he did it because his income was not adequate for the Garden Suburb or whether he thought his ideas might have more influence then on the population I do not know.

The surroundings were very monotonous, a small house, among many houses all built the same with a tiny bow window and a touch of stockbroker's Tudor above the main bedroom window just to give it 'class'.

In Uncle Charlie's house space in the steep roof had been made into a room of sorts and where the roof sloped down a kind of screen, you could hardly call it a wall, had been erected. On this was hung a series of brightly coloured posters, the captions of which were all in Russian. The pictures, as far as one could decipher them, portrayed rows of healthy, happy Soviet children marching forward into the future, while the others depicted drooping half starved children under the Capitalist system. This of course was not entirely without foundation, as we were to find out when the war came and evacuees from poor areas were sent from the big cities into good class homes. The posters were certainly vividly challenging, as my mother found when she unfortunately developed a bilious attack during her stay and had to be in bed in the room staring at them. Perhaps Uncle Charlie was a 'Communist Cell' for as Aunt Mamie explained the posters were there to illustrate Uncle Charlie's talks that he gave to people who came to hear him, but we did not really understand what it was all about.

After some years living there when old age loomed ahead, Uncle Charlie suddenly decided with practical insight to emigrate to his son and daughter-in-law in Rhodesia, as it was known in those days. A strange choice for a Communist.

He told the family he was not going to leave Mamie after his death to eke out a lonely old age in nursing homes like he had seen her spinster sisters doing.

It must have been an awful uprooting but it seemed to work, and when his heart gave way later and he passed away he left Auntie Mamie to live till her nineties, cared for by their family.

5

Chasing Lloyd George

My father's love of Wales and its comparative proximity to us in Staffordshire meant we went there for most of our summer holidays. The need to economise coupled with my father's deep attachment to the country meant that we took rooms on a farm in preference to the more usual accommodation let by seaside landladies. If it was a farm where the older members of the family spoke only Welsh, then my father was the more pleased, though as he did not speak Welsh himself this seemed rather strange. But he had this great attachment for the real thing just like in the realms of antiques he hated a 'fake', or what is now called period furniture.

There was one farm, for instance, where the old mother sat in the farmhouse kitchen almost like an antique piece of furniture herself and could not speak a word of English apparently but she would tell you proudly through her bilingual daughter that both her sons had entered the Church and were vicars of Welsh parishes.

My chief memory of that holiday was of our arrival at Aberystwyth in the pouring rain and having to bicycle eleven miles in it. The chief casualty was my mother's hat from Woodrows, a large and beautiful straw of rose-pink and brown, the colours in separate sections with roses made of pink straw all round the crown. However, as far as I recall the colour did not run and after being well dried it resumed its former dignity. But how mistaken we should think it today to choose such a hat for a seaside holiday especially when most of it was done on bicycles!

Llanon delighted my father because it was so remote, but my mother perceived that we children were growing up, and Ralph especially felt the need for greater sociability and more organised leisure activities.

It was arranged the next year that we should try to satisfy our varied needs by going to a farm on the outskirts of Criccieth, where Ralph soon found a tennis club he could join and yet my father could feel he was in reasonably remote surroundings on the farm. As I had not got to the stage of tennis in those days I was left a little by myself. Perhaps because of this I used to walk in the environs of the farm and came across a very odd piece of land at the side of it. It was rather boggy I think and had no normal farm crops on it but was mostly things like heather and little bushes. There were strange little round mounds covered with low but springy vegetation, and I felt instinctively that these were in some strange way closely connected with fairies of some sort. Whether they danced round them or lived invisibly in the tiny mounds I have no idea but I distinctly felt some presence of this kind there.

We were, however, very much kept in touch with the normal world because of the close proximity of the Premier, Lloyd George, whose bungalow house stood on the outskirts of the town. I recall viewing it quite easily when we passed by it up the road. It would nowadays be considered a very small and an unprotected place for a premier in office to live in.

A warship did appear suddenly in the bay, the *Valiant*, which became quite a holiday attraction on 'open days'. We were told it was a form of protection against the Irish but I could not quite see why since they would hardly be likely to arrive in an armada of boats. That was, of course, long before the bomb became an everyday weapon used by so many minority groups, and a tip and run attack was unknown, though I suppose a small boat would have been a useful form of getaway.

We very much wanted to see this great man since he only lived just up the road. My mother, who had to do the shopping every morning (to my dismay before we could go down to bathe) learnt from conversation with other customers that the best way to see him was to wait outside his chapel on a Sunday morning and watch him go in.

I recall that my father, though an admirer of Lloyd George, did not feel he should participate in this questionable activity. In those days clergymen always wore their uniform, a dog collar and a dark suit, though on holiday my father usually discarded his formal black cloth suit and took to an alpaca one. But to see a clergyman standing outside a Nonconformist chapel during Sunday morning church time merely to see a secular potentate was hardly dignified. So he went to Church and my mother led us on this adventure. We lined up in good time outside Lloyd George's chapel prepared for a splendid view. Presently a car came down the road and stopped at a neighbouring chapel before it reached us.

There was a roar of annoyance from the crowd, and everyone started to run. He had evaded us by going into his wife's chapel instead. Alas, we arrived at the door too late to see the great man in person. He had already slipped inside.

After that many of the crowd dispersed but we stood about wondering what to do. Some regulars went inside, and then an usher came to the door and beckoned us in. Hesitating, for in those days before the Ecumenical Movement became active you thought twice before entering someone else's religious citadel. We finally responded to the offer and walked inside.

The service was in full swing by that time and the Minister, or Elder for I don't think he wore robes, was delivering a very eloquent sermon evidently by the way he was waving his arms about and emphasising his pronouncements, but as they were in Welsh we did not understand a word of it. Only sometimes phrases would sound like some caricature of English and I had to bite my lip to suppress a smile. Of course, my mother having been seen by all the shopkeepers during the week in company with an Anglican parson, they soon recognised us as usurpers and I recall that we were the subject of severe scrutiny from the local tradesmen, and how many of them there were there clad now in formal black suits and bearing an air of dignity and superiority in their official places they had not shown us before. After all, this was their territory.

There was a clock behind the preacher and I kept on watching it when not taking a surreptitious look at the great man, who sat at the front but sideways to us, white-haired and dignified, absorbed apparently in the rhetoric of the sermon.

Of course in those days the ordinary person never heard a whisper of any affair with his secretary and dear Mrs Lloyd George in her best toque decorated with flowers dispersing her kindly smile generously seemed the embodiment of a faithful and supportive wife beside him.

The clock ticked away for an hour before the disquisition was finished. The rest of the service was soon over and we poured out into the street having endured an ordeal, but it was all worth it for the sake of seeing a famous person.

I shall always recall our last sight of Criccieth. We had made up our minds to get up early and have one more bathe before we left, we loved it so. Rather to our dismay we awoke to find the weather had completely changed. It was raining at times and there was a strong wind blowing which made the sea very rough. We were, however, intrepid bathers and the prospect of being knocked down by a few large waves did not deter us in the least. In fact we enjoyed it. Being buffeted about on a cold morning made you warm, and I recall how we came up from the beach, saying our last farewells, glowing, and how hot we felt when we got into the home-going train and passed into the stuffy environment of the country inland to return to the more mundane confines of the vicarage at home.

6

A Visit to Bath

It was a very good thing when Aunt Aggie repaired to Bath, because she found just the right little private hotel in Pulteney Street that gave her enough cosy comfort at a possible charge for her modest income.

It was a delightfully Edwardian place, with aspidistras in all the odd corners, and even a bit of a conservatory for proposals. It was inevitable, therefore, that all the other aunts and uncles, and they were a family of eleven, should hear of it, and decide to repair there too, the married ones with their wives and progeny, and the latter included my brother and me.

At least fourteen members of the family stayed there at different times. They were like some benign swarm of bees.

Aunt Aggie was always a pioneer, a sporting aunt we called her, a bit of a rebel up to her dying day, and she lived until well over seventy. Somehow she never grew old. She was always attired in what was known as 'Aunt Aggie's blue'. This matched her eyes perfectly, and in spite of her rather lined face, gave her an atmosphere of youth.

She used to cap these ensembles in summer with a large rush straw hat, neutral in colour, but with blue cornflowers woven into the front. One day in Bond Street, sitting at the back of cousin Joe's open Daimler, a dray horse mistook the hat for fodder, and put his head over the back of the car and started to nibble it. After that, she went in for a chiffon swathe.

Aunt Emmie came next, an elderly aunt with glasses and slightly prim look. She had done good works all her life. Austere to look at but when you got to know her, she had a great sense of humour, and was very kind and human.

I once had to spend the night on a sofa in her room at Bath. Both she and Aunt Aggie competed to lay shawls and blankets over me, topping up with a gorgeous plaid of Hunting Stewart. Of course, as the sofa was near the fire, I was far too hot, but I did not dare to complain about such kindness.

It was especially kind of Aunt Aggie to do this because she herself liked very few bedclothes, and was a fiend for fresh air. It was Aunt Emmie who liked things stuffy and warm. It was recounted in the family how once when staying with friends the two sisters had to share a bed. To Aunt Emmie's delight and Aunt Aggie's dismay, it was found to be a feather one. How were they to solve their problem with such differing tastes? Suddenly Aunt Aggie had a brainwave. She folded the feather bed deftly in half, Aunt Emmie climbed up on to the top layer, while Aunt Aggie slept below on the straw palliasse.

Aunt Aggie had one great problem due to her liking for unrestricted fresh air. She did not like to sleep with her curtains drawn, but found the early morning light hurt her eyes. But she had another brainwave. She made herself some wonderful blinkers out of brown paper. She fitted these delightedly on the first night, and duly retired to bed.

She had not been very long asleep, however, before she awoke again, and roused my cousin (with whom she was staying), with great urgency.

'Kay, Kay!' she cried. 'Someone has broken in. I can hear them moving about.'

'Nonsense!' replied Kay. 'I don't believe it.'

They paused to listen, but there was nothing to be heard.

'But I distinctly heard their feet going pitter patter, pitter patter,' she exclaimed.

They searched the house after that, but could find no-one, and so they went to bed again. They were just settling for sleep when Kay heard laughter coming from Aunt Aggie's room. She went to see what it was about.

'Kay, what do you think?' she said, 'All those feet, those pitter patters — it was my eyelids batting on the blinkers! I have just discovered it!'

Soon after this, Uncle Henry moved into a neighbouring vicarage. So he in a sense formed part of the colony because he was so often in Bath. He had plenty of time because he got a charming little parish near the Box tunnel where there were only about 100 parishioners, and he was little more than private chaplain to the big house there. He had rather good features, and a very fresh complexion; this with his white hair was most attractive and he had a slight lisp and a sort of Ralph Lynn-like capacity for getting into awkward situations. So he became quite well known.

The next one to join the family circle staying at the hotel was Auntie Annette, the eldest of the family who was used to taking command of the situation. She had blue eyes too. She was tall and very handsome, with rippling white hair. Both her sons were bishops, very large and jolly. It used to create great excitement when they came to stay, and took their meals in the small dining room at the hotel.

Philip was the most bulky and being a bishop in Australia he had a particularly friendly hail-fellow-well-met type of approach to people. Soon after his visit to Bath he became centre of attraction at his wedding in Sussex. That is the only time I have ever travelled with five bishops in a coach — a charabanc as we called it then — and one of them was an Archbishop.

We were bowling along excellently and the Australian bishops were introducing their wives to their various English friends when the coach halted outside a country pub. Imagine my embarrassment when out of the main door came Uncle Henry, talking in a very loud voice, and shouting goodbye to his friends where he had stayed the night. Being a little deaf he did not realise perhaps how strident his voice sounded, and leaving a pub after a good lunch, some people probably imagined he had eaten and drunk too well! I soon saw the reason for his jubilance, however, when he announced to the company that unfortunately he had had to leave his wife at home because she was not well. It was very seldom he was let off the leash, and he was behaving rather like a bouncing puppy!

Douglas, the other bishop, had very typical ecclesiastical features and figure and having spent all his life in England was a little more reserved and remote but a great favourite also with the guests of the Bath hotel. In fact as both the Douglas brothers were scholars of Winchester and of New College, I think they were all somewhat dazzled by them.

The hotel guests were a strange mixture. There was a tight-laced, rather imperious old lady like Mrs Pattinson, who, it was rumoured, had been a singer, but probably on the music hall rather than the concert stage. Her extraordinary black dress, was cut low and heavily trimmed round the bosom with scintillating pearl buttons. She was rather proud of it.

When dinner was over and the curtains were drawn, then bridge was played with great avidity and sparkle. Their conversation was loud at first like a lot of birds settling in their roosts under the eaves in the evening. Once settled the twittering ceased and the silence was broken only now and then by a few laconic remarks from one or other player.

Their faces were very stern and earnest as if they might have been playing for some high stakes and even Mrs Pattison did not go in for her usual dramatic 'declaration' as she did

84

in most situations, but might be said to be keeping her cards very close to her chest as the saying goes, that is as close as her large bosom would allow. I generally went to bed before this intense exercise finished so I never knew unfortunately who was the winner, but as one never heard any disturbance or even glimpsed any feeling between those taking part next day the closure must have been quite amicable.

It was in the morning, however, that we all felt the real zest of life when we set off to the irresistible Mecca of Milsom Street and the shops. There would often be a cold tang in the air, with a clear light over everything. How this weather outlined the grey, architectural beauty of Bath, those fascinating layers and layers of houses, rising upwards along the hillside like a series of strange ladders. 'Bath is the tea cup, Cheltenham the saucer,' the aunts used to say.

Perhaps to suit my father's taste, we would stroll round one of the wonderful terraces first, so perfect in their architectural entirety that it was a joy to feast the eye on them. The Crescent was a special favourite. Then we would drop down to the teeming crowds in Milsom Street, and the delights of the dress shops there, and the antiques which my father loved so.

Having looked, and my mother and I perhaps having fallen for some feminine frippery in one of the stores, then we would repair to a cafe, famous for its biscuits, and sit watching the buzz of Bath residents as they gathered for coffee at eleven o'clock. In no city, perhaps, were there so many personalities, people who were extraordinarily unusual, but felt so part of that city of individual character that they belonged to their surroundings and never became isolated eccentricities.

Most people came back for lunch at the hotel, after which we used to repair to the Pump Room, walking there via the Abbey precincts. I always remember the beauty of that part. It was linked in my mind somehow with an exquisite picture in Beatrix Potter's book *The Tailor of Gloucester*, though her picture was of another cathedral city, of course. Inside the Pump Room we sat quiet for a while, and I can still hear the soft noise of the water in the fountain as it bubbled up. I thought it tasted very nasty when I took some from my father's glass and I was very disappointed in it, since its fame had made me anticipate something very pleasant, in keeping with the social activities of Jane Austen's characters.

Our main objective, however, after lunch,

was the concert room. Of course, my aunts and uncles turned out in full force. As they were all deaf, they sat in the front row. This was very unfortunate because they had not long been sitting there before inevitably they all fell asleep. Some of them with their heads dropping forward, some of them back, but whichever way it was they were sure to snore, very loudly and lustily, with their mouths open. The result was a deafening chorus almost as terrific as a percussion band and most embarrassing to those of us who belonged to the family.

There was an interesting if accidental acoustical experiment when the orchestra played the famous 'Surprise Symphony'. The effect was instantaneous just as the composer intended. They all woke up with a bump, and a united snore. But at least it woke them for the rest of the concert.

We used to enjoy the tea in the interval very much. Aunt Aggie had an inexhaustible taste for Bath buns. Perhaps that was why she used so often to remark, regretfully to my mother, 'Oh, Alice, I feel as if I had swallowed the piano but never mind, I enjoyed it.'

It was not, of course, a formal meal at separate tables because there was really no time for that before the music began again.

87

We all sat round a bar counter where tea was served and the inevitable bath bun. There was a huge plate of them which ran up and down the counter rapidly. My mother took one and started to eat it but paused and laid it down while she listened to something one of the aunts was saying. Imagine her horror when she looked back at the counter only to find this partially bitten bun had been somehow caught up on to the plate full of them again and an old colonel at the other end had taken it up and was just about to start eating it!

He might never have noticed what had happened previously to it and merely taken it up and devoured it enjoyably in perfect innocence if my mother had not spoken, but honesty was inherent in her nature she could not keep silent.

'Stop, stop!' she cried. 'That's my bun, I have bitten it!'

Consternation ensued. Conversation came to an abrupt halt and the delinquent bun was passed back to my mother distastefully.

Though conversation was gradually resumed the atmosphere did not become totally relaxed until the bell went for the second part of the concert and everybody got occupied in the united effort of resuming their seats.

When the concert was over we would

stroll round the corridors feeling something of the past glories of the Regency Period. What famous beaux strode about here. What romantic and often frustrated ladies were involved in the social activities and through them sought to achieve security for the future, for in those days when there were no careers for women or pensions, marriage was an absolute essential for the middle classes. Jane Austen's characters, though fictitious, seemed to come alive then.

After this we descended to a lower layer in the building and an earlier period of history. What were these vigorous Roman occupiers like who came here and built such handsome dwellings, even installing central heating when it was unknown in England. As we walked round the pool and gazed into it my mind was full of these queries, but its dark mysterious waters did not give any clue, nor the fine stone figures that guarded it evince any reply.

But all good things come to an end, and finally the time would come for us to take the road home to Father's northern parish in a world of mines and pit banks, so different to the gentle west country.

I can recall especially one glorious October morning and the first frost of the year, as we climbed slowly in the car, from the 'tea cup', its grey severity softened by an early morning mist. On the heights above we watched the sun break through on the dazzling sparkle of a frost-covered landscape, lighting the leaves of red and gold on every tree, and the cream stone of the Cotswold houses bearing that mellow quality of peach-like bloom, which is the precious characteristic of their stone.

7

Total Eclipse

An interesting celestial event occurred in my school days, and I was lucky in being caught up in this major event because, owing to the increase of mobility and action, we were able to travel several hundred miles to view it.

In the summer of 1927 there was to be a total eclipse of the sun. There was a great deal of talk about this beforehand and the best place to view it from. One of the staff at my school hit on what seemed a daring idea then that she would take a limited party of girls from the school to see it at Southport.

The party had to be made up of girls who had no public exams to take that summer and whose work therefore would not suffer from the diversion. I came into that category. I was in Lower VI Special, ominous name because although I was better read than most people below the VI Form Standard my French and arithmetic were almost nil, and it had been decided that I should not even try for School Certificate, but be put into Lower VI Special.

Unfortunately I was subject to very bad colds and a barrier was put in my way by my house mistress, the great E.H.L. — who could seldom be moved — she thought that it would be very bad for me to go because I should catch one of my colds and be off work.

However, I argued I was tough. I came from the north and caught colds through infection *not* cold weather. I wrote frantically to my parents about this and somehow they were able to get me accepted as a member of the party. This opposition had only made it seem all the more exciting. When I found I was accepted for it I wrote a letter to my Mother about the expedition couched in such delicious Angela Brazil language that I have included it verbatim in this story.

It is indicative of the psychology of those days that I am so awed and amazed at having left the strict environs of my boarding school that I should be still wearing the uniform, and in company with the staff be charging through London at what seemed to me the wickedly late hour of ten o'clock at night. It was unbelievable!!

My mother must have been staying with her brother at Milford on the edge of Cannock Chase. It was there that the main line express trains, (steam in those days) emerged from the Shrugborough Tunnel with a roar, a tunnel so called because it ran past the famous mansion of that name owned by the Earls of Lichfield, the present one being better known as Patrick Lichfield, the photographer.

In this letter I allude to this location and on the return journey succeed in waving to my mother who is standing at Uncle Ernest's bedroom window, evidently prepared for the train passing by.

> 'Barry House
> High Wycombe
> Bucks.
> Sunday

'Darlingest Mummy,
'Thankyou so much for your letter.
'Yes it was lucky I just saw you that day I am so glad I got up and went to the door. I was just about to begin on a rather belated breakfast of bread and butter and raspberry jam having been waiting for it ever since I left Southport!! I never expected you would be there. It was clever of you to get the time of the train from that porter. It made me quite homesick to see all those places again. We stopped at Crewe for some time and saw the little

Stoke train just opposite us, but no one in it I knew. Then we went through Woore and Madley, and came into the Stafford line at Norton Bridge. There was hardly a soul on Stafford Station. After Milford I got too interested in breakfast to notice much!! Some people I had brek with were very struck with Shrugborough and asked who it belonged to.

'Well I must tell you all about the eclipse. We had supped here at 7.20 and then we were supposed to go and work but E.H.L. asked us to get two small suit cases to carry some things in, and so we took all the time over that nearly, not feeling very like work. We had to take books to read jerseys to sleep in, and our own sponges soap and towels, which were a great boon, as we got so dreadfully grubby. E.H.L. was *so* excited and bucked I have never seen her quite like it. She even insisted on our having her tiny clothes brush which she used for travelling and treasures greatly. We left the house with E.H.L. waving from the doorstep, while numerous people in pyjamas were gazing surreptitiously out of the dorm windows with looks of envy. We walked down to the Abbey. We did feel mad, walking through the corridors at nearly nine o'clock in our outdoor things just setting out somewhere. We went to the entrance hall, where every body was assembled and we got a packet of chock and a packet of biscuits each. Then we went off to the station. Miss Moore (who took us round the school when we came to look over it) was head of the expedition, and she was simply topping, not a bit fussy, she never got worked up or tried to do things in a stiff way. She just let us enjoy ourselves to the utmost. Each house had a staff to look after them, we had Miss Crawford. She is a Botany and Science mistress. I don't know if you remember her. She came up on my train to Marylebone that day you and all the cousins met me. We saw her going off in a taxi, plus bicycle. (She was *not* the one in my carriage) Well she was simply ripping. She is quite young and rather pretty, and again not a bit fussy!! 'The Stona' went too, a nice old lady who teaches geography. The Miss Cartwright went (she is a niece to the Wills at Bournemouth) Of course Bubbles (Miss Turner) went too, being the person who ran the expedition.

'We went up to London feeling awfully thrilled. We got a carriage to our selves. There were six of us. Lawrie did *not* go. She is not L VI and as she is in an exam form she would not get permission. Higgles went and Bats (the woolf) Sheila Forman (sister to the dimple) and Mary Geikie (Gory's sister) and now head of Barry and Molly Walker (that girl you said looked good natured) Bride's dark friend.

'When we arrived at Marylebone we turned out on the very same platform I came to last term. It was a very different 'alighting'!! I little thought when I should see that platform again how thrilled I should be!! Well we all marched off out of the station and started to walk to the bus. It was funny it was now after ten o'clock and London was beginning to look quite 'Nightish'. I don't think I have often been out in London so late. It did seem mad in school clothes and with school people of all things. We boarded a bus and went to Euston up Baker Street and Marylebone Road, and straight by Harley Street, Devonshire Place, Madame Tussauds and the parish church at Marylebone and York Gate where the Smiths lived. All very familiar places.

'We got off and found our way to Euston where we went on to the platform that we went from last hols. It was a gorgeous long train and it was funny to see all the crowd.

There was another special for Southport on the other side of the platform and the crowd was *immense* and so various. There were millions of nationalities all round, Indians, Chinese and Japanese, Jews etc, and such funny mixtures of English. A lot of young fellows who looked rather like shabby undergrads with haversacks on their backs, learned professors, oldish London business men, parsons and professional men, heaps of women, many sporting old ladies carrying sheaves of travelling rugs!!! and some rather common, sort of nouveau riche women who were going from pure curiosity, and lots of young girls.

'We all bought newspapers and settled down for the journey. We travelled in dining cars, but not used for eating; you know the sort of saloon thing I mean. We had tables to put our books on etc, and nice big windows to look out of. The other four Barrys filled up a seat of course, but Bats and I had to have a separate one and she narrowly escaped sitting on my hat!! The woman at our table had been kicking Bats, when sitting there and so she swore she would kick back. The woman came blundering in later and sat down kicking Bats again who lashed out in return, at this I started to laugh so much that Bats who was lying partly on top of me was tossed up and down like a indiarubber ball!!

'We dozed off again and I did not see anything more really until we reached Stafford, then after that we got to Crewe It did seem funny to think that we were going right by you while you were cosy in bed asleep. I wonder if we came with a great rush and a roar like expresses do, and if we shook the house as is usual. We stopped at Crewe and when we reached Wigan it was getting light. It was a dull morning almost like autumn and a bit hazy. The country was very flat and dull but you got a good view at any rate.

'We arrived at Southport at last. I *did* feel funny when we turned out on the platform I was not so physically sleepy exactly, but everything was in a dream and everybody seemed miles away. I felt as if, if I got tired of fighting through the crowd after Bats I could quite well just shut my eyes and sleep and wake up in my bed at school just like you do when you have a dream. We then went to a cafe and had a wash and some coffee and then we had to rush off to the station in fact I and several others did not get time for our coffee, but had to leave it there much to our sorrow!! However when we reached the station we had an hour to wait for the rest of the school as they made a mistake about the time. One poor girl felt sick, and so we left her behind and she came on with Miss Moore in a taxi and saw the eclipse all right.

'We took a little motor train to a place called Hillside about two miles outside Southport. There were great vast stretches of dunes for miles round and all those any where near the station were covered with people. The road over the railway bridge was black with people and the whole pavement lined with them and a stream of cars down the road. We went out on to a dune from which we got a good view of the sun. The sea was somewhere over to our left, and miles away and although we spent some hours there we never caught a glimpse of it once!!

'After a few seconds the sun began to get a tiny bit hidden like this. Then it went on increasing very slowly. The sky was a dull mauve, and there was a most extraordinary light all round like the beginning of a thunder storm. The sun was still golden and shining in a patch of light, but gradually it got darker and darker, and then at the last few seconds darkness spread like a great curtain. It sort of rushed along, and all the dunes round grew black as night, as if some awful calamity was over coming us. The people all sort of gasped with surprise, you could hear their cry travelling from hill to hill as they took it up. Then we slipped out eclipse glasses and looked at the sun, the sky was all mauve, and so was the moon which was hiding the sun, and on every side the light shone out in a narrow circle round the moon, a glorious yellow pearly colour. Then the moon raced off and the sky was lit up again although it took a long time to get off the whole sun it was incredible how short a time it lasted for a total eclipse I wish it had lasted longer. It was a marvellous sight. We *were* lucky in getting such a good view. It poured here all day and the rest of the school never saw a glimpse of it poor things.

'We returned to Southport again after walking on the dunes for a little and trying to see the sea. I believe we did see it a faint grey line miles away but it looked like just sky really. We came back to Southport with a weird couple (not of our party). They were a man and a woman, the man was a German about thirty while the woman was English I think, but they talked German hard all the way, occasionally she had to lapse into a word or two of English but talked German mostly, it did sound so funny to hear it talked. A bit later they started French and later Italian!! We got back and went to a Marks and Spencer Bazaar, a sort of Woolworth affair, where we sent off postcards to people. I think one of the most marvellous things about the place was the way in which everybody was up and about. There were crowds of people, at the station meeting people, and this place when we went for PC's was just full of people doing a roaring trade with a gramophone playing just as if it was about 11 o'clock instead of 6.30 a.m.!! We went and got some coffee at the cafe again, The Crawford was ripping and when we asked her how much our coffee cost she would not tell us and refused to let us pay, so Higgles gallantly seized a 6d and remarked handsomely, 'Oh well I will tip you then Miss Crawford,' and presented her with it, much to everyone's amazement!! We left Southport about 8.5. Unluckily we could not get nice seats altogether again, but Higgles and Bats and I had to share a two between us and so it was a bit of a squash!! However we dozed a bit being very tired, we travelled uneventfully and at Euston took a bus which took us right down the Upper Marylebone Road and up New Cavendish Street and then right across Portland Place, just below the Langham and then the way we came before, up Baker Street. At Marylebone we raided a fruit stall and spent a few shillings I am afraid and then we went to a cafe and had some cakes. Then we fell into a train and reached High Wycombe about 3.30.

'When we came here we all had high tea of eggs and jam and bread and butter etc., then a gorgeous hot bath and off to bed where we slept $14\frac{1}{2}$ hours or more, having breakfast at 8.30 next day. It was a glorious day. There was nothing to pay except the few shillings on fruit etc, so I am quite well off at present for money. I suppose it all goes on the bill.

'By the bye have you got those negatives? I do hope so did you send them to Sweetlands? I have not had any prints yet. Yesterday we played 2nd House. Isobel was in which rather surprised me but I thought she played quite well on the whole as far as her fielding was concerned. She was out first ball which was unlucky as it was a very sneaky bowl on the ground, but she got the chuck from 2nd House and Hardy was put in instead. I think that Ewen was rather annoyed at her running while fielding, she kept on remarking, 'Don't run on your toes like a blinking fairy!!' but it was hard luck her getting chucked. We lost. They were 70 for about 8 wickets while we were only 18 for 90. It was awful. The service is at 5 today so letters are off early so I must be closing.

'I am not going to the Mission this term I am afraid.

'Yesterday I had the most awful 10 minutes in the whole of my life. Everybody is being graded now and I had to play before the music staff, and I was so petrified I did not play one right note wasn't it awful. Miss Herron will *murder* me at my lesson on Wednesday.

'Kilmeny has had a ball on her hand, so she could not play in the match, also Laurie who had been sick and at the Hospice. It was a great pity.

'Only 3 weeks on Wednesday. Think of it!! Hip Hip

'Yes, it would be gorgeous if only you would have some tennis on Thursday after I come home. Do have any Ansteys Cliffords Lefevres and Dawes if obtainable *please*.

'Well I must close.

'*Don't* forget to tell me about the photos I do hope you have them safe.

'I do hope Daddy keeps well.
'I hope the pussies are well.
'Don't overwork your self
'Very best love darling to you all,
        'love
              'Ruth
'P.S. Does the Dr know any body called Bill Vernon at Oxford?!! I hope you like the long letter.

Please keep it it is so nice to look back on!

Please send this enclosure on to Harrods and send me the answer, as I can't get it E.H.L. or something one always stops Harrods answer!!'

8

Continental Adventure

It was Aunt Aggie who suggested that Mummy and I took a holiday abroad with her. At first we viewed it with trepidation, because we had never left these shores before. Any alarm about this must seem strange in these days when the Channel seems little more than a broad river and people cross it by sea or air in a few minutes, sometimes only for the day.

Auntie Aggie's invitation, however, finally seemed irresistible. Her blue eyes, her pretty blue clothes, and her sense of humour gave her a cheerful optimistic air. We felt we could not take the dangers of such an adventure too seriously.

My elder cousin 'K', who was somewhat of the same nature, was to accompany us. She had been quite a stalwart as a land girl in the first world war and ready to cope with anything. We had a photo published in the newspaper of her passing Buckingham Palace in a land girls' march carrying a live goose in her arms. Of course in these days we should all have protested about the poor thing getting frightened in all the traffic; in fact it would probably have fled before it reached there. But in those days it was only horses and carts that formed the traffic, so it probably felt more at home. Far less people could get off work or get trains to town to view the show. So the crowd was small and very obedient, waving politely to the Queen, not waving their banners instead in protest and support of some urgent cause as they do today. I felt if K could cope with London and a goose she could cope with a trip to France.

To add to the importance of our journey, as we were going to St Mâlo and Northern France we were not to take a short Channel crossing to Calais or Dieppe but to take a bigger ship from Southampton. This was not one of those great ocean-going liners that put into Le Havre, but something bigger than the little Channel steamer that served the 'poor man's crossing' to Dieppe for instance.

Another characteristic of a journey in those days was the amount of luggage you had to take. As far as I can remember my mother and I took a family trunk although we were only going for a few weeks' holiday. I know Aunt Aggie took a large hat box — but of that more later.

106

I chiefly recall having boarded the boat — we then settled into a large public cabin with bunks all round us full of prostrate figures preparing for the night. This struck me as very odd, having never slept in such a large open kind of bedroom before. Even the dormitories at school had beds well apart — with cubicle walls or curtains to separate us.

Everybody was saying it was best to get settled down before we came to the Channel Isles, as if we might encounter some horror like the Styx there. It was of course really that the current was tricky round the islands and the boat usually tossed about a lot to the detriment of all bad sailors. Aunt Aggie knew it all well.

Because of this stigma placed on them I never saw the Channel Isles as far as I can remember, and did not realise how this character of horror and fear belied them entirely.

The English took their night's rest much more seriously in those days, not having come in contact much with the Continental way of life and it was taken for granted that a proper night's rest was essential. I don't recall seizing on the opportunity of going up on deck to see either the sunset or the sunrise on the sea, as I do in these more travelled days when going to Norway.

Auntie Aggie was an old hand at the journey as she came to the same pension at St Servan, which was just outside St Mâlo, most summers. Such retreats were extremely cheap and helped to eke out the modest income of English spinsters in those days.

We were lucky however in having a quiet crossing and after we had been pushed and shoved through the Customs and passports, and chased up the porter with our heavy luggage, we found a taxi waiting for us. This was driven by a special friend of Auntie Aggie's, an Italian with an unpronounceable name. Why an Italian instead of a Frenchman we never knew. Aunt Aggie said he was so reliable.

Certainly he added variety to the scene. I have never had such a journey in my life in a car. St Mâlo was a lovely old walled town we had been told, but we seemed to see little of this as we tore along at a terrific speed through the most unexpected environs until it seemed like a dream or scenes you saw at the cinema, dashing across the screen.

On one occasion we seemed to be passing through the environs of a coal pit. There were the familiar hedge stocks and the trucks filled with coal and grime over everything. To our alarm, at one point, we actually drove along a railway line, terrified in case we should meet a truck coming down it. The only comfort was it was laid flat on the stone-covered area and not fenced like most railway lines so we could have left it in an emergency. I have never found out if there was a real coal mine at St Mâlo or whether the familiar equipment related only to a coal wharf at the docks but there did not seem to be any water there.

Our Italian friend tore along chatting happily to Auntie Aggie, having no idea apparently of the consternation suffered by his passengers behind him. We wondered when on earth the journey would end, when suddenly having come into a more residential area he turned the taxi abruptly into a right hand turning, so fast that he knocked a flamboyantly uniformed gendarme right off his bicycle. The impact was so abrupt that Aunt Aggie's huge round hat box of a sort of light wooden material, was flung off the pile of luggage, stacked up beside our driver, and went rolling off down the hill — irretrievably as it seemed at first.

The extraordinary thing was that neither the bicycle nor the gendarme seemed to be hurt and no notebook was brought out and incriminating details taken down. There seemed to be a friendly understanding between the two. Perhaps it often happened! Our hat box was retrieved and a few moments later we drove triumphantly into the gates of the pension. We had arrived at St Servan at last!

Behind the cosy white walls which surrounded our guest house, as they did most of the villas of St Servan, we formed a sort of world of our own. The garden was painfully tidy and unimaginative in comparison to an English one. No one ever seemed to go into it, except on one occasion when the whole French family, who kept the place, foregathered in the hen run chattering at a speed and highpitched tone that outstripped any real clucking hens. We puzzled over the cause until Aunt Aggie who had acquired some French through her many visits to St Servan, explained that the cause of the emotion was that a rat had been seen in the hen run. Nothing was apparently done about it and after a long time the human clucking ceased and the tempo went back to normal and the family returned to the house.

The other guests were apparently all English, except for a few mysterious French people who came and went very rapidly and did not register in our minds as human beings at all somehow.

In those days when it was so cheap to live abroad such places were peopled with redundant old ladies many of whom made a permanent habitat of the place. I chiefly recall in this case Miss Mead. Having met Aunt Aggie on many previous occasions she took a sort of proprietary interest in us and kept on nosing into our conversations and offering advice.

For instance when she heard my mother and I expostulating on the beauty of milliners we had visited and the exquisite soft straw hats in black we had obtained for a modest sum she interrupted us by saying in a heavy voice, 'You ought to go to Germany for hats. You will get them far cheaper there!'

It was no good explaining that the fare would be expensive, the style more teutonic and we had not any wish to go to Germany at the moment. Nothing would alter her judgment course however and so she failed to see the practical facts in this reply.

St Mâlo proved to be a glorious old walled town, untouched by war in those days, with narrow streets and fascinating shops with all those little French touches which were new to us. We scurried about, half in awe of it all while the great bell boomed from the magnificent cathedral.

It was then that I got a quite new

111

conception of Christian customs. Old peasant ladies in black with white shawls round their heads carrying buckets came in to say a prayer en route from their work. How very different this was to the 'Sunday best' Protestantism we practised in those days. The old peasant women had a daily life relationship with the Church even in their working clothes. Imagine if my mother had taken her mopping bucket with her to our church! It gave me something to ponder on! This relationship with real life had its drawbacks, however, we came to see when after a huge Confirmation Service with queues of child candidates the ensuing parties that the families held got rather out of hand late at night judging from the noise and sometimes the quarrels that broke the normally peaceful night. It was rumoured that the children stayed up for them (a strange habit since the average child in England would be tucked up in bed by then under the care of Nanny) and it was said the children also took wine and got drunk, though whether the rumours were true I never knew.

We excused all this by saying that the Bretons were a primitive people and therefore were apt to do these things. We were not to know that the noise of their celebrations were mild in comparison to the noise of a discotheque which carries for miles when the modern young are having even a normal dance here in England.

Besides French milliners St Mâlo had some charming lace shops. In those days when one had time to sit down to a nicely laid meal in the dining room, not in a super but bare kitchen, the sets of lace mats were irresistible, just the thing for our old oak dining table. I still have them tucked away in a drawer in the tallboy and to handle them is to bring back that holiday again and the exquisite delicacy of the French craft. They are scalloped mats with tiny roses made out of the same material.

My mother and I being great lovers of the sea, were not content only to view these urban beauties. I recall one glorious summer day when we travelled out by some means to the Pointe du Gruoin and from its lofty height viewed the glorious blue of the sea off that part of the coast of France. I thought the colour something unique that I should never see again but I was later to discover it in the glories of the Atlantic in North Cornwall.

Our sole companion in the long grass we sat in on the French headland, was a small goat and her kid. They appeared undisturbed until a foolish passerby wanting to make some comic gesture, since language proved an insuperable barrier to conversation, picked up the kid and brought it to us. The distress of the mother was so terrible we hastily signalled to him to put it back, which he did, but I made a vow from then onwards never to wear kid gloves, because behind their production was such distress and sorrow for the animal.

Later we descended to the more realistic surroundings of Cancale, a typical French fishing town with rows of innumerable small boats, rather untidy and not too clean resting before they put to sea. There was a wide esplanade to walk along flanking the quay for they were not great high boats that needed a dock, but one's progress along this was impeded by paraphernalia for winding in the boats etc. and greasy patches from this and the catches that had been landed there.

Our more frequent expeditions to the sea were however made by a ferocious little tram that snorted down from St Servan, deposited us at some point on the outskirts of St Mâlo as far as I can recall, and at this point a shrill voiced conductress would shout out, '*Changez pour Paramé*'.

The phrase became so familiar that it became a household word as things do and on many occasions we utilised it usefully at home later.

The intricacies of the French currency were quite beyond my mother, but she used to put her very large handbag on her knee open and let my cousin delve into it picking out all the right little bits to pay the fare with. In fact on one occasion as my cousin proudly asserted she had actually detected a mistake in the change given by the conductress and after an argument in broken French with her proved she was right and got the money back for us.

It was during this holiday that we met one English family with whom we became permanent friends. They stayed at the same guest house and like us sought the beach, in their case for the sake of the child. They were an Anglo-Indian major and his wife and their remarkable little daughter, Mildred. In those days the British had an Army in India and the fact that life was considered unsafe for white children after a certain age and the journey which had to be made by sea, which took a long time, caused many harrowing separations in those days between parents and children.

We grew very fond of this intelligent responsive little girl of only five years old who was constantly joining us, on the beach or in the guest house.

They had come back to leave Mildred

in an English school in spite of her age, because they dared not have her with them in India any longer. I think that this parting overshadowed things. We kept in touch with them after we all returned to England. The major went back when his leave was up but Mildred's mother stayed on for a while living near the school where Mildred was ultimately to be left as a resident — and in order that she should get used to it as a day pupil.

But the daily parting became such a traumatic experience that her mother decided that she had better make the final break and place her there as a boarder and return to India.

Why was Mildred so upset by this parting which in those days would seem normal to a child brought up in India from an early age? Did she foresee what was coming in the future or did her tension and distress cause the illness to develop and take a fatal turn? We shall never know but soon after her mother left for India Mildred developed an acute appendicitis with unusual complications and she died at St George's Hospital in London after an operation there.

Our attempts to get to know French people were not very successful nor very enthusiastically pursued. We accompanied Aunt Aggie on some of her expeditions to old haunts which involved meeting them. I remember her washerwoman best. In those days there were no launderettes available, or washing machines at home so a good washerwoman was a very important factor. The French are great artists at this and dry cleaning also. I suppose that the delicacy of fabric and their tendency to have things 'frilly' makes them practised in the art.

The only drawback to Aunt Aggie's washerwoman was that she did not speak any English. As long as one kept to the straight and narrow way of conversation about familiar objects involved in washing it was all right, but striking out into other fields led to complications. For instance when Madame politely asked after Aunt Emmie and inquired why she had not come also, Aunt Aggie replied to the astonishment of the lady, that her sister was not a good mattress.

On enquiry why it was necessary for her to fulfil this function, the mistake was discovered. Aunt Aggie had of course meant she is not a good sailor, but the two words are sufficiently alike to be easily confused.

Another of Aunt Aggie's expeditions was to her favourite café to partake of a *Baba au Rhum*. She had constantly regailed us on stories of the delights of this experience, the flavour being to her mind so good and juicy. In those days cakes were mostly English ones that we made at home and we had never met this delicacy in our own shops as most people have now. Imagine our dismay when presented with what seemed to us a damp spongecake that did not appeal at all to our palette. My cousin whispered to me that it tasted like bread out of the sink! but of course we could not let Aunt Aggie know that.

No, on the whole we did not acclimatise to France although through my grandmother's family, The Fourdriners, we are really of French origin. Back on terra firma, we felt that we were unlikely to leave these shores again for a long time.

9

Stonewall Country

Although we lived on the border of Derbyshire when you got right into the county there was a very different feeling about the whole area. As if preparing you for it outside Leek you climbed up and up and the hedges disappeared and the stone walls stood out rather stark and grey in comparison.

There was that exciting place called 'No Man's Heath' where the county borders all came together, Staffordshire, Derbyshire and Cheshire. The police were empowered to operate only in their own county so that a highwayman fleeing from justice took refuge in this place and just stepped over into another county when he saw the police coming after him! Just a stone wall to get over not a Berlin wall. There was nothing like Interpol either, or Extradition warrants in those days.

The Cat and Fiddle, now a fashionable pub to go to for motorists who skim up and down the hill to it in their fast cars just for a drink, was probably a cosy and inaccessible hostelry for such personalities, but even now in modern times we hear that it is entirely cut off by snow sometimes.

Buxton seemed a rather stern imitation of Bath although it was a spa and built of grey stone somewhat on the same lines. Perhaps I missed the amusing and friendly family groups that enlivened Bath. However I recall that when I went to Buxton it was with one of my contemporaries who had a grandmother and grandfather in rooms there pro tem. They must have had a great sense of humour, for when we arrived they were still chuckling over a faux pas of Grandma's. Having poor sight she had written a letter with some considerable effort and then looked for some blotting paper to blot it on, those being the days before biros came in and such a thing was necessary. Seeing a nice flat white object which she thought must be a desk top — she was not used to the new sitting room — she applied the letter to the imagined blotting paper only to find it was the top of Grandpa's head as he was sitting in a low chair! However, luckily he too had a sense of humour and it was handed on as a family joke ever after.

This part of Derbyshire was not all stone walls or severity. There was the parish of Tissington where they still carried on, probably a pre-Christian rite, that of 'Dressing the Wells'. Such an abundance of flowers and children decked with them. It was observed so meticulously each year.

It is so strange how these oases of traditional ceremony and celebrations have remained in isolated spots all down the ages. Why should they be there and not others? Were they, like No Man's Heath, some pocket of security for a people who did not wish to obey the current laws of the land and escaped the christianising of the country, or were the representatives of the Christian Faith there meticulously careful to follow Pope Gregory's instruction to St Augustine that the pagan rites should not be suppressed necessarily but when possible blended into the Christian ones.

The beautiful edifice of Tideswell Church known as the Cathedral of the Peak would make this latter theory more relevant. There was a beauty and exhilaration about that high plateau on which those two landmarks stood. I recall one particularly beautiful day when we strayed over there in search of a trail laid for a treasure hunt and how delighted I was to have this incentive to view it all even if we were travelling somewhat rapidly about in a car.

The part I got to know best, however, and

the local people, was down in the Dales. Of course we had visited Dovedale as a famous beauty spot many times. But that is what Windermere is to the Lakes. The dale where my uncle had his fishing lodge was one of great depth and in the old days somewhat cut off. The local people had lived there mostly all their lives and were individual personalities locally known.

My first memories are of my uncle's river keeper and his wife, the Bartrams, who later moved up into the village. What a strikingly good-looking old lady she was, with her white wavy hair parted down the middle and drawn back off her brows into a bun at the back. Though her husband always wore rough tweeds to suit his occupation, they had a kind of neatness about them almost akin to a military uniform. They were both deeply respectful to my uncle as their employer, not in any sanctimonious way. They had been brought up to be so. His needs were their concern. How it cushioned life in those days to have such people around.

I became aware of a very different relationship to that of most of our parishioners and my father. They came asking advice and help from him, or my mother, and I don't recall that the little maids in the kitchen were

My garden outside the nursery window, dominated by an old brass sundial, before it was fully planted.

An early photo of the author in one of Nanny's beautifully made smocks.

My brother and I on one of many holidays on the Welsh coast.

Aunt Nellie, a handsome elder sister, confident of her future.

Little Alice, whom the family thought no one would want to marry.

The Lathkill Lodge, the old cottage of Derbyshire stone with the typical Edwardian wing and balcony hitched on to it.

Those steps at Haddon Hall down which Dorothy Vernon stole away to the fulfilment of her romance.

My mother and I on the beach at Polzeath.

A picnic on the beach at Daymer Bay near St Enodoc and where my friend saw the visionary procession.

St Enodoc, the once buried church showing the strange tower inside which the light appeared.

Hitler with his strange hypnotic eyes staring into the future leaves a special performance of the play at Oberammergau.

A charabanc ride round Cologne before we came home from the Oberammergau tour. When we asked the driver if he had voted that day in the election for the Party, he replied, 'Yes, my insurance ticket,' and showed us his membership card.

Alois Lang, who took the part of Christ, resembled our mental picture of Christ so closely that it was strangely disturbing to encounter Lang carving wood in his shop.

The fjord was rippled just like the sheen on velvet as we sailed by the sleeping town of Tromsoe and caught our last glimpse of the Midnight Sun.

The graceful lines of *Meteor* anchored on the peaceful waters of a fjord while Norwegian farmers and a typical fjord pony assist in gathering the hay which must be spread out on sticks to dry.

Crummock Water with Mellbreak and the surrounding panorama of mountains on to which our little hut looked.

Mother and daughter.

very aware of our needs. We tried to poke them up about things instead, but Nanny made up for it all.

The village above the lodge was called Over Haddon. Its essential function was very much a family affair and the Bartrams' daughter kept the village post office, a plump capable lady who used to appear through a door that led into the living room.

She also had a girl to help her, a very splendid girl, Mrs Bartram said, but she added in a low, rather apprehensive voice, 'I don't look to see her there very long because she is courting strong.'

In those days friendships leading to matrimony did not develop hastily and something rapid was a matter for comment.

The road down to the Lodge was very steep and it zig-zagged around to reduce the steepness of the descent but this only made it the more alarming to drive up and down it for fear for some reason you could not get round one of the corners.

The house consisted of an old stone cottage facing the river with an Edwardian wing of red brick and a white verandah hitched on to it facing down the Dale.

Everything inside was very luxurious in a quiet bachelor way. Impeccable beds, first class blankets from Maples and Worcester china of a soft tawny brown and gold design with exceptionally big breakfast cups for the coffee over which one seemed to linger a long time — for Uncle Ernest took his time off in a slow dignified way.

The river was very beautiful. Immediately by the Lodge it went underground and was covered by a carpet of lush vegetation and bushes, but known to be a treacherous place to walk.

Below the house it came out in a lovely stream and was dammed up into long pools of smooth water that lay like velvet under the overhanging trees. Water rats inhabited the banks, suddenly swimming like half submerged submarines rapidly towards their holes for cover. Little dippers flew and then curtsied as they perched on overhanging branches rather cheekily, and watched one fishing.

How often I was reminded of Rupert Brooke for whose poems I had a particular admiration then. I especially recalled his reflections on fish because it seemed to make them individual personalities and caused me ultimately to give up fishing.

Fish (fly-replete in depth of June.
Dawdling away their watery noon)
Ponder deep wisdom, dark or clear . . .

Oh! never fly conceals a hook,
Fish say, in the Eternal Brook.

Fishing went on, however, for the moment and later when Old Bartram retired up to a cottage in the village he was miraculously replaced by his son, Herbert, a person with an equally ideal wife. Why were we so lucky in those days?

Herbert had left the Dale in the first world war and joined the Navy, since his knowledge was of things pertaining to water. He used to tell me how he was on a ship going to Murmansk when it was so icy that the men's hands, presumably in gloves, used to freeze to the guns and the new crew would have to defreeze them before they could move off duty.

Herbert returned to the peace of the Dale safely when the war was over and devoted his time to the river again. It was a remark of his born of his individual knowledge of each fish that altered my attitude to them; he said; 'It is no good you casting for that fish, Miss, because your uncle pricked him two days ago.' I realised he even knew most of the fish as individuals and what was more, they evidently could feel pain, this proved it. It was soon after this that becoming a vegetarian I gave up fishing altogether.

It was of course a wonderful incentive to stand still and enjoy the beauties of the river and I only discovered this through fishing. Yet why must we depend on this incentive, this occupation which disrupts the quiet peace of the pool and tricks its inhabitant into thinking that it has caught a real fly when really it is an artificial one concealing a deadly hook? Such treachery is so unnecessary. Why can't we just stand and stare at it all in peace and quiet instead?

It was not, however, always so quiet in the Dale. Sometimes a whole charabanc load of human beings would arrive, people out for the day from Sheffield not very suitably clad, for in those days leisure clothes had not come in. Some of the women wore satin blouses which horrified us! I think I even saw a bowler hat one day.

My uncle who was really a very kindly person at heart would sit on the verandah as a new group filed past, and murmur as if only for himself to hear, 'I'd like to shoot the lot of them!'

After that the hikers began to come. They were more aware of the country code but completely naive about the habits of wild life. If they saw a fish they would stop and point at it and call out to my uncle, thinking he would like to know and come over and catch it!

They seemed to have no sense that the creature had by then darted right down into the depths of the river bed for safety, being scared by their demonstration and most of the other fish had gone too.

That hikers were scarce in those days is borne out by an extraordinary conversation I overheard my uncle have with an old friend who lived most of the year near Stornaway in Scotland. Every summer she used to come south and open her house for six weeks and invite all her friends to a huge garden party. It was on this occasion that she enquired from my uncle as to how his fishing was going.

'Oh, pretty well,' he replied, 'but we get such a lot of hikers in the Dale now and they frighten the fish.

'I don't expect,' he added, 'that you know what a hiker is?'

'Oh indeed I do,' she replied in great solemnity. 'I once had one on my place! I got my Ghillie Murdoch to lock him in the servants hall until the police came and took him away.' And she added with scorn, 'He wore a kilt and he came from Glasgow!'

There was something of this private

landowner's feeling about the areas round the Dale for although there was a right of way up it which no one could stop, if you took the foot path on the far side of the Dale where there was no road yet you found it hedged in by immaculate and impenetrable fences with many notices calling attention to the fact that it was private property and trespassers would be prosecuted. The overhead trees were very lovely and the view gazing into the woods but you could never be part of them, never sit down on the carpet of cool green if tired. It was like being in a spectator queue at a famous art collection that was roped in at either side and forced to move on without touching anything.

Having mastered the energy to get up the hill one came out of the woods onto a beautiful plateau. Large fields bounded by stone walls and a big farm in the distance. The feeling of greater space and freedom was exhilarating.

This was the land of the great farms which this part of Derbyshire had a lot of. They were mostly inhabited by a sturdy people, residents of the neighbourhood, motivated by local traditions. I was not to know then that I should become a neighbour and friend of Alison Uttley who came of such stock and immortalized the people and their way of life in her many books starting with *Country Child*.

The village above the Lathkill Dale on the other side was called 'Over Haddon' a most unusual prefix, instead of the more usual Higher or Upper. The title must date back a long way to another village of the same name, but now extinct, called Nether Haddon. The only traces left of that are those of the old church now incorporated into the family chapel of Haddon Hall. What happened to that vanished village? Did some lord of the manor pull it down in order to raise this edifice instead?

To me Haddon Hall was the embodiment of romantic beauty with its soft grey walls and pink roses clinging to the stone, and the steps down which Dorothy Vernon is said to have eloped, so appropriately set in the centre of the scene as if for a theatre set.

When my mother was young a play was produced based on the story. It was one of the first theatres she was taken to when growing up. So caught up was she in the romance of the story that she was oblivious to her surroundings, until Granny, sitting a few seats away down the row, called out to another member of the party in a loud voice, 'Tell Alice not to sit with her mouth open.'

This brought my mother back to earth with a crash!

The love story of Dorothy Vernon is one of the most famous because her elopement and marriage were only achieved after so much anxiety and perseverance. She was the younger daughter of Sir George Vernon, the owner of Haddon Hall and a very rich and powerful man. Dorothy was very beautiful with long red hair, and as a biographer observed, 'She bewitches in a single glance.'

There were of course many suitors for her hand in marriage, and her father planned to arrange her marriage to the one he thought most eligible. Dorothy, however, fell deeply in love with the second son of the Duke of Rutland, John Manners, and he with her.

Sir George thought a second son was inappropriate for such a prize, since he would not inherit the title or much of the wealth. Moreover there was an ancient feud between the two families. Somewhat similar to the story of Romeo and Juliet, the two families in this case were divided by past allegiances to Mary Stuart and Elizabeth Tudor.

John Manners' request to pay his suit was refused therefore and the couple forbidden to see each other at all. They devised a way, however, to defeat this ban and to meet secretly, thanks to the help of Will Dawson, the head forester who gave John Manners work. Dorothy was in the habit of going riding. So no one suspected that she was going to meet John Manners in the woods.

Dorothy was very fond of her father in spite of his domineering and unsociable nature and these conflicting loyalties worried her. Sir George Vernon decided that his daughter should marry the Earl of Derby. Dorothy and John therefore decided that they must speedily elope. Luckily her elder sister was to marry and this led to much gaiety and a party the previous night, at Haddon Hall. Will Dawson provided horses and food for them at an arranged spot and at dead of night, when the revellers were still occupied with the celebrations, Dorothy stole away down those now famous steps, to meet her lover.

After a terrifying ride lasting two days and only stopping to change horses fearing that the search party her father sent out would catch up with them they reached Aylestone in Leicestershire, where they were married at last. It proved a very happy marriage; the only sad thing was that Dorothy died comparatively young, leaving four children for her husband to bring up.

I remember Haddon best the last time I saw it in the twilight of a late autumn day with a thin mist like veils of tulle swelling up from the River Wye that encircled it. All that was missing was the soft music of a string orchestra and the sounds of revelry within and the shadowy figure of a ghostly Dorothy Vernon slipping down those steps to join her lover waiting with his horses round the corner. Stern Stonewall Derbyshire has its romantic moments.

10

Strange Episodes in Cornwall

I discovered Polzeath a long time ago. Parking the car was a problem even in the 1930s. We had just put it at the end of a row of houses on the front at New Polzeath because there was no sign to say you could not do so, when a charming little lady appeared.

She explained that it was forbidden to park there really, as it was the entrance to her hotel. In those days the day visitors were kept very much at bay and observing this law meant putting the car at the top of the hill and carrying all the paraphernalia down to the beach, but of course we complied.

'Good gracious,' she said, 'do you know you are the first people I have moved on who have ever been polite about it!'

After that we became firm friends. This was 'Mrs Mac' whose home had always been in Polzeath. For a time she had become a well-known actress on the London stage, but love intervened, she became the wife of a local solicitor and settled here again. She was a friend of the famous actress sisters

Irene and Violet Vanbrugh and wanted to ask them down to enjoy the beauties of Polzeath in between engagements. So she took two cottages on the sea front. That was how her hotel Atlantic House began. It was a very nice one, the only drawback was that you were expected to change for dinner and we followed the rule just like being on a big liner out of loyalty to the 'Captain' so to speak though it was a great effort to come in early to do this on a nice summer night.

What would Mrs Mac say now if she saw fat grey-haired ladies taking tea in the lounge in a skimpy bust bodice and only a bikini to cover their lower parts. One can hardly say it is a pretty sight.

There were quite a lot of things to do after dinner for which evening dress was not suitable. Watching the Green Flash, for instance, when the sun went down over the sea. The flash came only at the very last minute so you had to wait outside for it for some time, quite chilly in evening dress.

Then there was the fourth bathe of the day. Surfing was a very important pastime then because there were few rival occupations. What a fascination there was about choosing your wave and leaping on to it (lying on your board), at the very right moment so that you were carried up the flat sandy beach as far as possible. How satisfying when you felt you had struck at the right moment, it was as good as a pilot must feel when his plane becomes airborne. Sunbathing had not caught on like it has now. We bathed three or four times a day. The last bathe took place by moonlight if possible or in the dim light of a summer night. I recall a party coming down there and driving the car over the sand down as close to the sea as possible.

They did not realise it was wet underneath when they parked it. In the morning when we looked out of the window we were surprised to see a long black object just protruding from the sand. It was the roof, all that was to be seen of this large Alvis car parked there last night. Luckily no one had got sucked in with it and later some men came with a tractor and hauled it out again.

That was the time that we stayed in a house next door to Mrs Mac's hotel (I don't know why) because I recall one of the ladies who lived there saying somewhat caustically, 'They probably only do it to get the insurance money!'

They were two rather unusual old ladies like so many people in Polzeath, not the quiet seaside landladies we imagined sinking back when the PGs had left into a quiet rural life.

They had a Bentley Sports Car, we found out, which they kept more or less hidden away till the season was over, and then they brought it out and tore all round the country in it!

It was in that house that I had the strange psychic experience during sleep, of becoming completely weightless and seeing a huge ball of golden light. What Cornish saint might have dwelt on that site before modern man came and destroyed the atmosphere?

Mrs Mac was a great believer in the folk stories of the neighbourhood. Brought up in a house almost on the beach in Old Polzeath over by Tristram's Cove, she spoke of the Mermaid there (who is said to have tried with her magic powers to lure Tristram down in the depths of the sea) as if she was a real person and how she used to hear the Mermaid sobbing at times. Local tradition said that out of fury because of her failure to get Tristram into her domain she had thrown up the sand bar which suddenly appeared across the Padstow Estuary and wrecked the whole of the fleet of sailing boats from Port Quin leaving it a deserted village.

When Mrs Mac's aunt lived with them as an old lady she used to sit out a lot on the cliff and when she came in she would say, 'I heard marvellous music all day out there.' There seemed no normal explanation of this. Mrs Mac said that all this sort of thing disappeared when the tourists came. They destroyed the atmosphere.

However there are the modern innovations more suitable for restless contemporary travellers today. The Malibu Boards, for instance, a great drawback for surfers as they take up so much of the sea. Then there are the inflatables, in spite of the warning that the latter are not safe and should not be taken out to sea. I suppose that's why the Council have got life-savers now with their sharply coloured flags out on stands on the beach, making it look rather like an outpost of the old German Empire, for I have never known anyone get drowned at Polzeath through 'natural causes', and we never had life-guards before.

But it would appear that even nature has an innovation for us, a phenomenon I have not seen till recently. Sitting on the beach at low tide by the Blow Hole one day I was surprised to see the other side being invaded by a strange 'mist'. Was it spray? Moisture from damp sand with the sun on it, or even sand? It was travelling at some speed blown by the wind which was coming from my side of the beach and it went up to some height. Thinking this side of the beach I was on was lucky to be without it I walked up to the shops.

The strange thing was that when looking back the part of beach I had come from it was all enveloped by this phenomenon too, but you could not see it when you were in it, only perhaps 50 yards away. No wonder people on the other side of the beach whom I had just seen showered by it were apparently indifferent to it, they also had no idea it was there at all.

Was it a symbol of our modern world's illusions about which we are constantly being warned that they will consume us if we don't realise their reality? George Orwell's forecast, warfare, devouring robots, etc? But how could people enjoying a wonderful day at Polzeath come to realise this?

Still in spite of these changes so long as this world exists, Polzeath will always remain the same. Pentire Point is always there with its glorious shades of light as the shifting clouds and the sun light passes over it and there is the evening light on the Padstow Estuary from Daymer Bay. Those island rocks look immovable, which you first see on the horizon as you descend the hill into the Polzeath, the familiar landscape again full of anticipation at viewing it.

When we had not the energy to climb

the heights of Pentire Point and view the wonderful coastal scenery that the walk along it reveals, with the intense blue of the Atlantic and the seals coming and going in the rocky caves, we would turn the other way over the low cliff top, level and covered with springy turf, and come to Daymer Bay, and the tiny village of Trebetherick where the poet John Betjeman lived for so many years, and the Church of St Enodoc where he is now buried. No wonder he wrote that poem about it. 'Blessed be St Enodoc.'

There is something rather mysterious about Daymer Bay though the many people who come there to enjoy a bathe and picnic on the beach may not notice it. Its formation is strange to begin with. Sheltered from the Atlantic gales it has a lush vegetation that is quite different to other parts of the immediate coast. Although it is low-lying and flat Bray Hill suddenly rises up out of the estuary, something akin to St Michael's Mount, though no one has ever built on it since the barrows of the Iron Age. It is said that when it was excavated ancient coins, possibly of Roman origin, were found there. We used to walk to the top and view the strange formation which showed signs of it having been a fortified point.

A friend who was given the loan of a hut

near the beach to stay in told me of a very strange experience she had there. She woke in the night and heard singing gradually getting nearer and nearer. She was not in a dream state apparently and she could not understand why the girl friend who shared the hut did not wake and hear it too.

She realised gradually that it was a procession of people carrying lights who passed by, until the music faded away in the distance. She saw this vision when down there as a teacher with an evacuated school. There was an enforced black out at the time of course so it cannot have been some local celebration. It must have been something from the past. My friend was a person of integrity and practical nature, not the kind of person who would imagine it.

The only clue I could think of to give her was by quoting Tennyson's poem 'The Lady of Shalott'.

And some times thro' the silent nights
A funeral with plumes and lights
And music, went to Camelot.

The lowlands are used as a golf course but in the middle of this with paths leading up to it marked by white stones, is St Enodoc known as the Buried Church because it was for a long time covered by drifting sand and then dug up again.

That itself is of an unusual shape, the tower forms a small transept off the main aisle half way up the church, not at the west end as most towers are. Was it some watch tower put there in pre-Christian days to defend the place or guide the ships out at sea? I had a strange experience there.

I had often visited this church and had seen in past years a simple wooden cross hung on the wall in the little transept off the nave of the Church. On it was written Captain Morvan, Mort. RIP. I imagined it was a cross set up by some French peasants when he fell in France during one of the world wars and that the captain's body had been later taken into a War Graves Cemetery and given an official cross and that this one had been brought home by his relatives. But I have never heard of any relatives living there.

One summer night when spending a holiday down there with friends, we went in to the church quite late at night. I think it was about 10 p.m. The door had been left partly open and Hugo, a member of the family who went on holiday with me, whom I was with, pushed it open and strode up to the altar saying half jokingly, 'I hope the

141

Saint will walk.' He was a Catholic who often visited Italy and always said that visions there were an everyday occurrence.

If only he had not strode up to the altar so quickly he might have witnessed what I saw. A light seemed to come out of the wall on the lefthand side of the transept and go over to the right where it fell on the Cross. I am not sure if it faded there or went through the window. It was a light with a point and a tail as far as I can recall but it took me with surprise. It was something like the light that a rocket leaves in its track.

I told Hugo about this of course at once, but he had not actually witnessed it himself unfortunately.

I queried car headlights as being the cause but when I mentioned it to the local taxi driver who took me sometimes to the train home, he said he had often taken ladies wanting to go to a service there to the nearest point a car could go, and at no point could a car come near enough to cast its headlights into the transept and provide what might have been a natural cause for this.

Unfortunately the Cross has broken up with the years and there are only a few bits left; the transept is now the vestry. I did mention it to a vicar after a service some years ago but he said he had only just come, and knew nothing of local things.

What strange influences are there around this district? There is a well just above the church and in the parish of St Miniver which is said to have had healing properties in the past; the procession seen at night by my friend passing her hut; and the Light on the Cross that I saw in St Enodoc Church. Surely there is some great supernatural power here?

143

11

We Discover Oberammergau

It was a good many years before we went abroad again. Our visit to France had confirmed our view that foreigners were quite different to us, a strange alien race while the English were the only normal people and England protected by the Channel the only normal land.

There was however a link with something that cut across all these false barriers we built up and motivated us to make the effort to leave our island citadel again. This was the Passion play at Oberammergau. Here was a bible story being enacted that we could share in, something we had known all our lives.

Our bishop relative soon linked us up with a clergyman in a neighbouring parish who was taking a party mainly of parishioners but in which we were permitted to join. Thus hedged round by our fellow countrymen we felt enheartened to plunge into the unknown once again.

I think my mother must have been filled with apprehension about it all for I recall being in London before we joined the party, and she was feeling so ill that we went round looking for a doctor but perhaps mercifully we were unable to find one that night because her illness passed off.

In those days only the rich went by plane and we boarded the usual continental express at Victoria, crossed to the Continent and then began a long and rather weary train journey over land through Germany.

We had fallen asleep, a deep sleep it must have been for me, for I had forgotten where I was when I suddenly awoke and saw that the train was passing beside a vast stream of churning green waters, the colour of which I had never seen before. I can never forget that first glimpse of it, a stream that was to mean so much to me later. To add to my amazement every now and then the train ran through small towns with brightly painted houses, like Hans Andersen's Fairy Stories, things I had never associated before with real life.

Were we travelling in a child's story book land? The whole thing was so unreal that I wondered if I was still asleep.

With the incentive of this wonderful view my mother seemed to become much better and I remember we regaled ourselves on some coffee and sandwiches while we blinked

145

at the Rhineland passing before us.

Later on we came to the flatter lands and I was amazed by vast areas of green arable cultivation without any of the hedge rows that divided our English meadows in those days. But this open land did not seem like a prairie, as it does here perhaps because the landscape was dotted with cosy little farm houses and churches with long thin towers with little mushroom roofs on top, the whole covered with bright red tiles.

The final stage of our journey was done in a small local train, a typical mountain railway with all those amusing informalities which only such a railway can provide and which alas we have lost here with the closing of the branch lines.

At one of the large stations a man came down the platform with a tray round his neck laden with cakes and sweets. He spoke fluent English and as trade was not doing too well broke out in exasperation, 'Cakes and chocolates for sweethearts and wives. Come on, gentlemen, what is the matter with you!'

This brought a ripple of laughter from the stolid English on the train but I did not see any increase in his customers.

As the train climbed the vegetation got more and more lush, and the sunshine seemed brighter, our spirits rose in spite of the long journey.

The old guard on the train who mingled with the passengers like a bus conductor, made many friendly jokes so when he said 'Are you going to see Hitler?' we thought he was only joking and testing us out as regards our reactions to his name. This was in 1934 when Hitler had only recently come to power.

We smiled amiably and did not commit ourselves to any point of view. When we at last arrived at our destination we were far too absorbed by its exquisite painted houses and the crowds pressing along the village street, some of them clad in the picturesque *lederhosen*, to remember what he said. We found that we were staying over the village bakery with a family called Rutz, cousins of the then famous Annie Rutz who took the part of the Virgin Mary in the play. The smell of new bread was very good.

It was only when we had unpacked and settled in that our landlady asked the same question. 'Aren't you going to see Hitler?' 'Yes, but where?' we asked. 'Just down the street,' she replied. 'He has been to the play and will be coming out of the theatre any time now.'

Amazed at this we set off at once in pursuit

of this famous man. We found our way to the main entrance to the theatre, where there was only a small crowd lining the pavement. Oberammergau was never very enthusiastic about him, although he came from only just over the border in Austria and built up his movement in the Beer Halls of Munich. In Oberammergau they were occupied in serving the real God and feared the power of this secular one who might seek to alter the play. It was rumoured to suit his views that all the best people including Christ were Nordic. Presently there was a stir in the crowd and Hitler appeared. Stepping into an open touring car he stood with his hands on the back of the front seat just behind the driver.

There were no bullet-proof cars in those days. If someone had realised his significance then and shot him history would have been totally different. But good seldom comes out of violence.

As I stood and gazed at him in amazement hardly believing he was really there, I became aware of one thing. He was not the scruffy little sergeant major with a small moustache that the British papers portrayed in their photos of him, but a much more dangerous person, an extraordinary personality, who had eyes the like of which I had never seen before, for although he was facing a crowd of so called admirers he gazed ahead of him with a fixed stare like someone in a trance, yet in spite of this lack of movement his eyes had something hypnotic about them. They were fascinating, they held you by some unseen power.

My practical self, however, saw in him an object like a rescued stray dog or a battered baby, something that had been beaten, ill-treated and humiliated, and therefore distrusted all mankind.

According to a *Sunday Times* article much later my impression was correct. His father beat him ceaselessly. In fact so much so that on one occasion his brothers thought he was dead but he was revived again somehow. My feelings towards him were of compassion therefore, not misguided admiration or even antagonism.

What a strange leader to have and yet did he not symbolise Germany after the first world war, beaten, humiliated, starved, deprived of a normal government? Did the Allies not create the exact soil which would inevitably be implanted by a dictator, telling a people worn down by their conditions what to do giving them back a sense of purpose though it was the wrong purpose, and ultimately aiming at vindicating their defeat by endeavouring to conquer all Europe.

In those far off days in Oberammergau we could not see all this panorama of history, and when Hitler had passed through the almost silent crowd, for only about one hand went up in the Hitler salute, we forgot all about him, caught up in the extraordinary activities of this village life.

How did this now world famous community remain untainted by the adverse elements of publicity and the opportunity to make money if they wished? Never yet have they succumbed to the temptation to be filmed. Perhaps because of its sure foundations; the production of the play was founded on a promise made hundreds of years ago as a thank offering to God for an answered prayer. When plague broke out in the neighbourhood the village of Oberammergau enforced a *cordon sanitaire* around the village but one man broke it by slipping in unseen to visit his family. He developed the plague, and an epidemic broke out.

But the village gathered together and prayed that if God would stop it spreading they would perform a Passion Play every ten years in the village. Their prayers were answered, the plague stopped and the great play was instituted which has influenced people with its spiritual power for hundreds

150

of years and attracted people from all over the world.

These two episodes, the conquest of the play and the conquest of Hitler seem to illustrate so vividly the effects of good and evil acts, and their escalating power. It is like the rings that spread when you drop a stone into a pond. The bitter retribution after the first world war and the coming of Hitler, his character affected by his personal suffering and humiliation alas found root in post war conditions.

The united efforts of the villagers in Oberammergau invoked the power of prayer to control the epidemic of the plague that their combined action generated. 'These (devils) are only cast out by prayer and fasting' we are told in the Gospel.

Hitler's tragic life terminated in the Bunker in Berlin and most of his followers with him, their military conquests firmly defeated but Oberammergau lives on and its spiritual power will survive down the ages.

Perhaps one of the most important foundations of the play is its naturalness. A play done by people of the village, not augmented by any professional star imported from outside, and this attitude appears to generate extraordinary natural talent among the people.

Moreover they must live the life of the person they are portraying. For instance, when the actress chosen for the part of the Virgin Mary, was seen kissing her fiancé, a young Munich doctor, good night, she was severely reprimanded by the authorities because although it was a perfectly respectable action for her to take as his fiancée, it was not considered an action relevant to the behaviour of the Mother of God.

Another important point is that they do not use any make up at all, but rely on their natural complexions, which are of course, luckily very good from the effects of the mountain air.

It was in Oberammergau that I first learnt to be tolerant to men with long hair, especially the boys who tore about on bicycles, like most boys do, in rough tweed suits, with their hair flying out in the wind. Far from deploring them as hippies one felt admiring of them because they had gained the privilege of being included in the play.

Besides the ban on greasepaint the scenery is of the most simple structural kind and the back cloth is not an imitation of nature by the brush of an artist but an opening in the wall at the back of the stage which acts as a frame to a perfect presentation of the mountains and the green slope leading up to them.

There is no roof over the area for crowd scenes; the players must accept that they are at the mercy of the elements. Sometimes the chorus were standing drenched with heavy blinding rain which only a mountainous country can produce, but quite undeterred they went on with their act.

Of course the robes used have no restrictions, they are all glorious in colour, and when appropriate sumptious for King Herod for example. To see these glorious garments all hung up in vast cupboards to fit them takes a very long time and is part of the visitors programme.

The village comes alive about 5 a.m. I shall never forget the first morning being woken by the gentle tinkle of cow-bells and going out on a verandah which overhung the street, flanked by window boxes painted blue and filled with pink geraniums all lit by the brilliant sunshine of an early morning in a mountainous village.

Everyone was very early in doing the milking because in those days it was an obligation for every player to go to daily Mass, in spite of the fact that they had to take part in a play which went on from eight in the morning till six o'clock at night. There were two thousand of them so the players, plus the many visitors who wanted to be present, made a huge congregation. To add to this an orchestra also took part in the Mass beside the choir making altogether the most marvellous volume of music. Not only the High Altar was ablaze with candles and activity, but all the little side chapels containing a similar altar had a priest celebrating Mass in order to cope with the enormous number of people wishing to receive Communion.

When this amazing event was over we went home for a quick breakfast consisting of those wonderfully crisp rolls which seem to belong only to the continent, and strong coffee.

And then the play began in the huge theatre with its open front. Perhaps one of the most extraordinary experiences of one's life was to see played out the familiar bible story by actors who were so real and dedicated that it seemed as if one had stepped back in time and was actually living in Palestine. It is said that one of the actors who took the part of Judas was so enveloped in remorse that after one performance he went out and attempted to kill himself, but was luckily prevented from doing this by his friends.

In 1934, Alois Lang took the part of Christ while his father, the previous one, became leader of the chorus. Of all the actors I have seen in the part, Alois Lang was the most moving, the most similar to my idea of Christ. It was uncanny to go when the play was not on, and see him at work in his shop carving wood, for appropriately he too was a carpenter, so like in appearance was he to that of Christ.

The fact that the play was not done in a language we understood seemed irrelevant in fact. In some ways it was better since we knew the story so well that it came over to us through the senses rather than the ears.

Sometimes it seems shattering to view these scenes at the human level, for we have kept them too much in cotton wool, too rarefied we forget that Christ had to face the realities of life under a foreign dictator.

When we left Oberammergau we all felt I think that we had had a unique experience and become the wiser for it. Since then I have been back several times; it would be wrong to say it had become a habit, but rather a method of spiritual reinforcement.

I have been to see the play, and I have been when the play is not on. Then I felt Oberammergau was rather dead because the villagers, perhaps sensibly, do not court public gaze. They keep within the confines of their homes. There is no primitive village pub left. The travel agents have made them all into tourist hotels. Alois Lang owned one of them when we were there, but he lived in a house nearby where he could sometimes be glimpsed in his orchard that surrounded it, when the play was not on.

Upon the Korfel the highest point in the range of mountains in which Oberammergau nestles, the Cross stands supreme still, for in spite of this inevitable sophistication, which had been brought to the village through becoming world famous the real roots of Oberammergau still stand firm. The integrity of a promise to give a Passion Play every ten years as a thank offering for the delivery from the plague still holds good.

When the war came I put a picture of the High Altar in Oberammergau in my prayer book and prayed every day, 'That is Germany at her best. Make all Germany like that.' Perhaps some of that power generated by all the prayers said then over the years bore fruit. We have a united Europe, a stable Government in Germany, not a nation humiliated and separated by bitter Allies. Now even France, the old enemy, is co-operating with Germany. Can we not hope that this may spread to the whole world?

12

My Initiation into London Theatre Life

The stage has always had a fascination for me ever since I was, as a reluctant self-conscious schoolgirl, drawn into a drawing room performance of Thackeray's *The Rose and The Ring*. I was a considerable failure in it for I recall at the dramatic moment when the identity of the character I was representing was called into question I had to say, 'I have no relics but this baby shoe' and produce the object from my bosom with a dramatic gesture. Imagine my horror when I plunged my hand down there only to find I had left it back stage! In spite of this faux pas, I felt an awareness during the play, of a kind of power over people, a chance to hide behind someone else's facade and implant my personality through them on to the audience.

There was another play I took part in at a somewhat later age. The chief episode I recall there was when the hero forgot his part — no fault of mine on this occasion — and he had to go on embracing me for a most immeasurable time trying to remember it while a would-be suitor (one in real life, not the play) had to be held back in the wings so overcome was he with jealousy at my being rapturously embraced for so long.

However it was mostly as an enthusiastic member of the audience that I linked up with the acting profession after this. We had a wonderful theatre near us, the Victoria Theatre, Hanley. Then I viewed such stalwarts as Julia Neilsen and Fred Terry, and their son Dennis Neilson-Terry with whom I fell completely in love as Mr Tawnish in a Jeffery Farnol play. There were also Sir Frank Benson, Arthur Bouchier and many others who put in an appearance in that ancient plush edifice.

It was therefore with considerable interest that we learned that my mother's elder sister was going to marry her cousin Rupert Lister, a professional actor. I had known of him for some time and we had actually glimpsed him when he came to Cromer when we were on holiday there and acted in the charming play *Raffles*. He was on tour and it must have been under very difficult conditions because at Cromer it was held in some schoolrooms or mini town hall and the props must have been borrowed locally for an old gentleman sitting behind us kept on shouting out in a rather outraged voice, 'My whisky! My decanter!' and banging on the floor with his stick. Having lent them, it seemed strange he was not content to sit back and enjoy a reflected glory in silence.

The story was about a gentleman cricketer, Raffles, who turned to crime, but burglars behaved like gentlemen in those days and they never carried shotguns to bang off at people and terminate the scene. Rupert Lister was a very good-looking man and he appeared really very handsome in a beautifully cut suit with his wavy grey hair brushed upwards and back off his face. He had at the end of the play to make a series of escapes. I recall how in the last one his handsome profile had stood outlined in the narrow space that opened before us in the flap of a door. That was the last we saw of him I think until he appeared in the real role of an uncle in our family.

Aunt Nellie had been the handsome one of the family. She was supposed to have many admirers, but no one seemed to want her for life. There was the story of the Englishman in Africa who was coming home to marry her but died mysteriously on his way down to the coast — perhaps murdered by his servants. It made a tragic story to tell, an unfulfilled love on which to focus, but my mother always said that even at that time she was sleeping with another man's letters under her pillow. In those days girls seemed to do this strange thing; perhaps they hoped to get romantic dreams from the proximity, since no one but the most reckless would think of sleeping with the man himself before marriage.

Such was the dominating image of my aunt as the prize bird that when Granny, sitting at their Edwardian breakfast table (at which Grandpa typically read *The Times*), broke the sacred silence by remarking, 'That young clergyman, George Plant, has been coming here a lot lately. I rather think he has fallen in love with Alice', Grandpa, without showing the slightest reaction or sign of surprise, said, 'You mean Nellie', and went on with *The Times*.

But the unexpected did happen. George Plant did marry 'little Alice' and Aunt Nellie remained a spinster till she met her widowed cousin quite late in life.

I came across some of my mother's letters written to my father when they were engaged. I have included extracts here although it means going back in time, because it shows the relationship and habits of an Edwardian family, quite frequent in those days. Also it shows the great modesty of a younger daughter and her wish to please the man she had fallen in love with, only to find after many years that my father had now fallen in love with her. My father was 38 before he married. This was not so unusual in those days when a man was expected to have an assured position in life before he asked anyone to be his wife.

This letter shows the feeling almost of shame that a girl of her social standing felt at having left boarding school at sixteen years of age. Those were the days when most of them went on to a finishing school and only emerged as young ladies. Her mother had finished in Paris, being the daughter of a rich businessman in London.

My father, on the other hand, in spite of being one of a family of eleven and the son of a poor parson, had succeeded in going to Oxford and taking a degree, quite a rarity in those days.

My mother's father had earned no money; he had tried once unsuccessfully to farm, it was said. Although he had been genuinely in love with Granny, he found it very convenient to use her money largely for his interests, keeping, for instance, nine horses in the stable for hunting, an occupation which he did not approve of for women and in which Granny did not indulge. This letter reveals how he had sold or was planning to sell the only horse suitable for her carriage and was letting them walk up from Grindley Station, an indication of things to come. As there was no Married Woman's Property Act at that time, he was perfectly within his legal rights to do this and she had no power to bring a complaint against him other than human selfishness.

The letter also shows the care and consideration that children of those days, especially daughters, were expected to give to their parents. One of them must be always at home, because it was so dull for mother when her devoted son, Ernest, was away at the solicitor's office, working hard to rise to partnership status to get more money to help her.

My mother's school fees were paid by Granny's father, so that when he died my mother had at once to come home and become another prop in the family circle to help out with the problems when the servants left — which they often did even in those days — mostly because of my grandfather's irascible temper.

In spite of the fact that they did have a staff of servants, Grandpa insisted that one of his two daughters was home every afternoon to pour out his tea when he came in from hunting. So the sisters, invited to any social event, had to decide which should go and I think it was often 'little Alice' who stayed at home.

In these days when everyone is encouraged at the earliest age to 'do their own thing', the contrast is immense and the loss of family unity very apparent. But this letter shows how parents often exploited that loyalty and makes the modern trend in the other direction seem apparent. The great thing is that affection should over-ride any convention either way and link the family with a real bond.

Park Hill
Chartley
Dec. 10th 1903

My dearest George,

Mother and I arrived home quite safely yesterday. We were not met at Grindley, so walked up, and were very sorry to find on arriving that Father was riding the cob round the field, showing him to a gentleman who had evidently come over with the purpose of buying him.

We don't know yet if he is sold or not; but as father seemed rather conciliatory in his manner at supper last night, we fear he is. It will really be an awful shame if he has sold him he makes such a capital harness horse for Mother's brougham.

Mother and Nell have gone into Stafford by the 10. train, and return by the 2. So I have had a nice long morning all to myself. I have been very busy making pastry and now at 12.30 I am writing to you hoping I get a fairly long epistle finished before lunch.

When I first work I thought I was at Dilhorne still but when I remembered where I was I was so sorry. I must thank you, dearest George, for all your goodness to me. I can honestly say it has been the very happiest ten days I have ever spent in my life. You don't know how comparatively light all the home worries seem now I have you to live for. The one and only thing that makes me wish we could be better off is, that I don't like to have you talking about giving up your hounds, and not being a mason any longer, and things of that sort. You seem to spend little enough on yourself as it is, and I know what a pleasure those beagles are to you. I do hope George you will find you can keep them after all.

I do think I shall be able to make your money go further in the house than it does now, as I did notice Mrs Tomlinson was rather extravagant, and there is a great deal in knowing how to use things up and make the best of them if one wants to keep one's butchers' bills down, though you must not think I shall be mean over the housekeeping and not provide enough. By the by I wonder how the beagles would like me keeping poultry. Do you think they would take the chickens?? I shall be so happy in trying to make your home as comfortable as I possibly can, and at the same time practising economy. I don't think you will find you have got a worret for a wife, as although one does get worried here often, I think I can truthfully say it is not my nature to do so.

I really think I am perhaps the most easy going of the family. I only hope when you know me better than you do now, that you may never be disappointed in me. I can't help wishing I were a better companion for you in many ways, but I will do my best George dear to make you a good tempered domesticated wife, if I can't lay claim to much education, and other talents or accomplishments. Neither have I ancestors or looks to recommend me, as some girls have in this neighbourhood. You know, you don't know my faults, and perhaps see me at my best, and I am not your equal in either brains or education by a *long* way as I told you the other day. I am afraid you will have a very great deal to teach me. I do so much wonder if your sisters will approve of me. I am afraid it is rather different liking me as a friend, to having me as a *sister* in law and I know how much they all think of you. I am going to ask you, if you will be content for the present, with a hand shake instead of a kiss before any of the others, unless it's mother alone. Please don't think me unkind asking this; but I do feel just a little shy before the others, and I would rather explain to you straight out, than I have you think me unkind in any way or indifferent to you. It seemed so funny to hear you telling me the other day you never could get me to say anything to you in the days when you were at Weston, because I was haunted for months after you left the neighbourhood with the horrid feeling that I had let you see that I thought a great deal of you, I evidently did not, though I suppose it was my fear of this that made me short with you.

I am very glad though you told me about yourself and, she being someone I know, I might have heard from someone else some day, and I should so have wished you had told me yourself. I do earnestly hope though George, that as far as you are concerned, I shall not be doing wrong by keeping to my yes on Thursday. You know sometimes I have misgivings that when you get to know me better, you may not find me the companion you think me. I know myself best, and I often feel what a very common-place individual I am. No George your confession does *not* certainly make me condemn you in any way. I too have had my small experiences, and must confess to a whole box of letters in my possession now, waiting to be burnt. I am afraid I used sometimes to compare the writer with yourself, and they have always got the worst of the comparison. Yes I want to come to Dilhorne very much again that is when it is *quite* convenient to your sister to have me. When I return home from Burton Nell wants to go away for a few days, so I must be here then, as one of us always stays with mother otherwise it would be so dull here when Ernest is away all day.

I am afraid Mother will have a lonely evening on Wednesday. Father still preserves strict silence with us all.

We have got a hired carriage and pair from Uttoxeter to take us and leave here at 8.15, picking Mr Jones up on the way, I expect. (Note, Mr Jones another curate was my father's rival now safely defeated). About Mother's anxiety about me on Thursday night. She was not really a bit cross, but, she is very apt to worry over trifles. It is all thanks to Father I am quite sure.

With all my love, hoping I see you on Monday.

Ever your loving
Alice.

She did do right to say 'Yes' on Thursday for so began a happy marriage and a united family.

Marriage was, of course, very important for a girl in those days since they did not have the outlet of a career. So the fact that my mother married young and my aunt did not was a bitter pill. It was because of this that I fear we children were a source of jealousy to my aunt. She always said if she had married in time she would have had five children.

It came as a considerable surprise therefore when I was in my teens and she asked me to London to stay with her and go to a series of theatres 'to initiate me' so to speak in the theatre world.

Our activities were mostly centred on the theatres in Shaftesbury Avenue. Uncle

Rupert was acting at the Apollo in *This Thing Called Love* with Robert Loraine. Strangely enough this play with such an intriguing title, as I was still at school in a very feminine establishment perhaps, did not interest me so much.

We went to several theatres during that short stay. I think that Aunt Nellie, left at home alone every evening while her handsome husband made love to other ladies in the play, was rather glad to have me as an excuse to attire herself in one of her fine evening dresses and all the jewellery she had inherited from Granny, and enjoy the delights of the West End. (She always got all her clothes at Bradleys, Westbourne Grove, the exclusive shop to which ladies drove in taxis for the privilege of purchasing their clothes.)

Her attitude to her own handsome looks was summed up when we were ensconced in our seats in the dress circle of a theatre whose walls were lined with large mirrors. Aunt Nellie suddenly remarked to me, 'Oh I was wondering who that handsome looking grey-haired woman was across the dress circle and I have just realised it's me!'

I was fascinated by the lights of the West End but Aunt Nellie who was used to being escorted by a male on most of her outings was very apprehensive in the street and against us defenceless females lingering for a minute to look at anything. Moreover she thought it was quite improper for any respectable female to walk up Shaftesbury Avenue in the evening alone. Any women we saw there she hinted mysteriously were sure to be 'ladies of ill fame'.

As it was too far out to have a taxi, (they lived in Basset Road off Ladbroke Grove) we had to run the gauntlet of these imagined thieves and prostitutes by walking up this 'disreputable' street from the bus which set us down at Piccadilly Circus. As a precautionary measure she would tuck my arm firmly into hers and then wrap her Paisley Shawl round her in a cocoon-like manner in order to hide her rings and set off on this so-called perilous walk.

Far from passing unseen down the street this Siamese-like conglomeration was of course bound to meet with disasters, when one person would have passed down the pavement easily two locked together bumped into people frequently. I was embarrassed by seeing many men draw aside after they had received a blow like a billiard ball 'cannoned off the cush' and look with amazement at this human bundle that could hardly be accounted for as some new form of soliciting from prostitutes.

Having done the journey home safely, one evening, I recall that we got off the bus in Ladbroke Grove (we had a long quiet road to walk down as Aunt Nellie's flat was at the far end). Cocooning herself again, we set off at a good pace, but after a while we became aware that steps were following us. We quickened our pace and the footsteps did also; we achieved almost a gallop but the steps were still following us behind and then just as we reached the garden gate, expecting anything to happen, we heard a laugh and a cheery voice say, 'I have been trying to catch you up ever since I left the tube.'

It was Uncle Rupert. She had been running away from her own husband!

After that there was a large meal, as actors are prone to take after the play is over, and much friendly conversation promoted by Uncle Rupert. As Mr Pepys would say, 'And so to bed.'

13

Going to Balls and Parties

One of the social activities in which I was expected to be involved as I grew up was going to balls. Such functions do still go on in limited numbers and are engaged in by those who choose to be involved but in those days they were all part of the normal programme for young people from the professional classes upwards.

This of course meant first obtaining a long dress suitable for the occasion and as these had low cut tops and often little more than a strap on the shoulder, an elaborate system of pinning had to be gone through to avoid other straps showing. This and all the matching accessories to be found and assembled led to much apprehension and frustration, and is aptly summed up in an old Punch cartoon of a policeman called to a burglary and saying to the owner of the house, 'It's plain to see as old 'ands have been at work 'ere, Sir.'

'Oh no, constable,' replies the owner. 'This is not the scene of the burglary, this is my daughter's room. She has just been dressing for a dance.'

I recall I had an apricot chiffon frock for my first long frock. I was rather fond of that one; it had a skirt made up mostly of frills of this material and it was reasonably short at the front but the frills sloped down almost to the floor at the back.

However, my choicest dress was one of pale pink taffeta with a long pale blue sash. The bodice was boned and tightly fitted to the figure and the skirt was made up of handkerchief points (falling like handkerchiefs if you hung them with the corner pointed downwards). The main skirt was of taffeta too but each point was edged with net that matched it exactly. An additional attraction about the dress was its origin. It was a model made by the Queen's dressmaker for Marie Tempest to look at among others. Then when she chose it, an identical one had been made to measure for her to wear in her play *The First Mrs Fraser* in which she was acting at that time. So I felt very delighted at having its original.

An inevitable addition to this evening toilette was a velvet cloak. Such a choice was not fortunate or practical because it only gave an appearance of warmth and seemed totally inadequate in contrast to a heavy winter coat worn in the day time. When most leisure activities are attended by young people in these days in jeans and a T-shirt, this evening toilette may seem strangely elaborate to them. Moreover one only arrived at such functions after a slow and rigorous journey, cars being less speedy in those days and car heaters unknown.

I recall clearly the first of my sorties into this social sphere, I suppose fashionable people would have called it my coming-out dance, but one did not use that term if a mere parson's daughter.

The ball was known locally as The 5th North. It never seemed to strike us to inquire further and ask 5th North what? On this particular night it was very foggy and going down-hill through a village we actually struck the kerb but seemed none the worse for it luckily, so we drove on. Outside the village we encountered a herd of cows being driven out to the field after milking. This was long before milking parlours with machines were kept in the fields, bringing the farmer to the cow rather than the cow to the farmer, so we crawled quite patiently behind them; in any case the fog was such that we could not go much faster.

Imagine our dismay when we were forced to come to a standstill because the farmer having fulfilled his task was shutting a gate across our route and preventing us from proceeding further. We had followed him blindly in the thick fog and never realised we had left the main road and driven up a lane which ended in a grass field.

The member of the party who was driving got out and asked the farmer if he could tell us the way to the 5th North. It was quite obvious that he had not got the foggiest idea where or what it was.

I began to despair. Would we ever reach this longed-for goal? Was all our dressing up and enduring the cold wasted? We seemed miles away from the urban surroundings of the town and the glamour of the dance. But somehow we got back on to the main road and the fog having somewhat abated, reached the fringe of the Five Towns as they were called, and finally the hall where the ball was held.

Its full identity was made apparent to me when I noticed two soldiers in full dress uniform standing at attention on the dance floor facing down the room. The dance was organised by the 5th North Staffordshire Regiment. This colourful tableau seemed a good idea, until one member of the guard becoming giddy watching the constantly revolving dancers and overcome with the heat of the room fell forward in a faint on his fixed bayonet which narrowly missed his jugular vein. He was rushed away by the ambulance man on duty, and as far as I can remember, the habit of putting soldiers on guard was discontinued completely when we attended the ball in later years.

Except for this disturbing episode, no further crisis occurred. All was bright lights and glamour and I became swept up into a swirling mess of dancers in a vast space where there was really room to follow the rhythm of the dance unimpeded and I began to realise the joys of that and why some groups of people make dancing a ritual.

My mother used to say much as she adored ballroom dancing she thought if she had ever learnt to waltz on ice she would have altered her allegiance. She thought that looked the best of all. My mother came out at another of the memorable social occasions which lightened the winter months, the County Ball at Stafford. It was really in aid of the County Infirmary, I believe, but I am afraid the aspect of good works was not to the fore. The word 'county' meant something at the top of the social ladder and everybody was determined to climb up it and be there if possible.

My generous uncle used to order about

eight tickets and invite me to bring my boy friends over from North Staffordshire. I knew quite a lot of nice young men there, parsons' and doctors' sons who lived locally and I found them pleasant to spend an evening with but none of these friendships went deep enough to make me wish to extend it to a state of matrimony. We had little really in common. The generation of the twenties and thirties were not interested in the problems of the world-wide community or the poor, not even in culture. It was considered rather 'cissy' to like poetry or music. Their leisure activities were mostly centred on the dirt track or the cinema — and those young people who were higher up the social scale in hunting and shooting.

Public School education was supposed to teach a good basis of decent behaviour founded on the classical principles of democracy. Originally everyone passed through this process. Even realistic disciplines like science were only just beginnning to appear on the curriculum under the title of 'the Modern Side'. It seems strange now when this subject plays such a prominent part in life and seems to overlap into everyday community life and the concerns of the ordinary citizen.

I sometimes think when I struggle with the

problems of finance, forms to fill in, income tax, the laws of the modern bureaucracy, what a pity my uncle did not put me for six months in his office to learn how to deal with all these matters instead of planning these social events with people whose friendship would not blossom into a permanent partnership. Learning to live on one's own, that is what I needed really for the future years.

However the ball was full of glamour and very pleasant as a diversion. The environs were particularly appropriate for it. The County buildings were built of an attractive grey stone, eighteenth-century in style with an open space paved with cobbles in front of them. We went in at a side door for the ball but it was quite a big and impressive one and opened onto an entrance hall backed by a beautiful staircase which led up to the ballroom. It was particularly suitable for showing off long dresses of a glamorous kind as the guests moved slowly upwards being received always by a grandee at the top which made most people feel important and they were satisfied by it though the greeting was only a formal one and only took a moment. You had to be careful, however, not to trip over your long frock which touched the step above you before your feet did, and fall forward in front of the hostess.

There was an amusing story going round how a mischievous young man on a similar occasion at a neighbouring ball had cleverly tripped up his partner just at the crucial moment causing her to fall forward on to the hostess's very adequate bosom, much to the poor girl's embarrassment.

We were each provided with a programme with a pencil attached and you strove to fill it with available young men because to sit out even one dance was embarrassing. Most people brought house parties in which the sexes were evenly balanced but as Uncle Ernest invited me to bring men friends my programme was soon full and they had time to ask girls in other parties too.

A few men who came did not dance at all. I remember one very solid-looking son of a neighbour of my uncle's sat around the whole night, and when another man asked him why he came at all he replied, 'Oh, I don't know, to see some chaps.'

This personified the majority of the men. They were only too glad where numbers allowed it, to take time off dancing with the ladies and have a good chat in the bar.

I soon found that the drawback of these functions was that the men one got introduced to who could dance tended to have the least brain, or shall we say the more superficial approach to life, and the men who thought more deeply about things tended to be more heavy on the feet and self-conscious about dancing at all. Where one encountered someone with brains and a sense of how to dance too, that was a great discovery and they were to be cultivated.

In those days one danced together with the man's arm round you, not in derisive little jerks and turns on your own, like people do today. So the partner did matter quite considerably.

The best balls of all that I went to were the Commem and May Week Balls, held in the summer at Oxford and Cambridge colleges, because they were held mostly in marquees in the most beautiful environment and the social atmosphere of the event seemed to fall into the background in comparison with the beauties of nature. I have never forgotten the extraordinary shade of deep blue that the delphiniums had in the slowly returning dawn in an Oxford college garden, nor the mysterious beauty of the tall trees in the Fellows' Garden (only opened on rare occasions) when one had entered by a path mostly guided by fairy lights, with candles placed in tiny glasspots along the ground;

there were no garish electric bulbs with red paint on them then.

We had gone to the Fellows' Garden because it had gone round the grapevine that the Junior Proctor could be seen there wrapped in a passionate embrace with his partner on a garden seat. Having inspected this phenomenon with my partner I found the trees far more interesting to gaze at. I wonder how many people made the trek over the Backs to the Fellows' Garden to observe this poor man who was doubtless only taking time off his normally austere duties.

There was the water, too, on which you could take a trip at any time during the night in a punt drifting under Clare Bridge or the other way, and all the time there was the sound of music coming out of the marquee and you knew that at any time you could step in there and enter into the dancing on a good floor with a first-class band. At no time had the delights of dancing found in a sophisticated life, and nature, come so close together for me.

Oxford might not have the Backs and the river close at hand to go on, but it had places like The Trout at Godstow for breakfast after the ball. How cosy its soft grey stone and ancient interior seemed after the chill of dawn in the college garden, and if the water passing by looked cold one could always recall the golden summer afternoon that Lewis Carroll rowed by with his young protégées and the story of *Alice in Wonderland* came to be told.

I seemed to get much more involved with various social festivities during May week at Cambridge because it happened that my friends were there, though my family were at Oxford.

I recall staying at an hotel in Cambridge, a rare extravagance because we usually motored back home after breakfast. It was near a waterfall, which was at the end of the comparatively small garden. I have never before tried to sleep close to the fascinating sound of a perpetual cascade of running water. The girl friend who shared my room tossed and turned all night so disturbed was she by it, but I think if I had been there a second night and alone I would have found this wonderful sound hypnotic and productive of sleep rather than the reverse.

We also attended the Varsity Theatre to see the much discussed play by James Elroy Flecker, *Hassan*, about the Middle East. I recall that it was there that I first observed this strange habit of some actors entering from the back of the auditorium and going up on to the stage.

Yasmin (the main female part) was taken by a particularly beautiful girl, imported from Oxford for her father was an important person in University drama there. We viewed the harrowing play, the procession of Protracted Death and the tragic execution of the Lovers with some concern but it had no reality for us. We did not know then that about fifty years later a film would be taken of a somewhat similar episode happening in real life, and shown as *Death of a Princess*. In those days the Middle East meant nothing to us, just a fairy story like the *Arabian Nights*. How far we have come since those days of balls and social functions being the main interest in life, and how have modern inventions in communications either by actual contact or visual pictures enlarged the canvas for our vision?

★ ★ ★

As well as the exciting events of a ball, we also had parties to look forward to. In those days, without television, these were the highlights of our social lives even if they were mixed blessings at times. I recently came across an account I wrote at the time of one such annual event — the Party at Pinhoes:

'On New Year's Eve we always go to a party at the Pinhoes. It has now become a kind of annual event. Did I say event, well perhaps that is hardly the term to use, perhaps I should have said ordeal.

'The Pinhoes are known to have the coldest and grubbiest house in the whole district but because the family are well known locally and are so very kind every one always turns up. As every New Year approaches we feel with a frenzied anxiety the time getting nearer and nearer, and almost begin to shiver before it has arrived. Sometimes we try to get out of it only to be dragged there by friends who are determined we shall not escape the ordeal they themselves are about to face.

'So we all don woolly garments under our evening dresses (the men wear pullovers under their DJs) and off we go; having said a touching farewell to our warm wraps in an upstairs bedroom and lingered in front of a gas fire (resembling in size a postage stamp) just long enough to send an awakening crinkle down the spine, we descend to join in the 'frivolities'.

'The first game consists of finding things which are not exactly hidden but disguised so as to appear invisible. I believe this goes by the name of camouflage. For instance a rapturous curve at the base of an ancient fire screen when prodded reveals an extremely mellow brown stocking wound round it with such cunning intricacy as to appear completely part of the structure. (It would not be any use of course doing this with any ordinary stocking as the colour would not be right.) The Pinhoes' stockings are exceptionally mellow. An ancient piece of gold bric à brac in the hall reveals, only after minute scrutiny, a mouldering banana which has wound itself cunningly into a gap in the discoloured gilt work with which it has a strange affinity.

' 'The Pinhoes' is a regular paradise for such a game as among such an inexhaustible supply of 'mellow' bric à brac there are endless happy hunting grounds. On your way round these objects you meet all and sundry with pencil poised and list in hand deep in the process of concentration. At first it is with a feeling of surprise that you come across several old gentlemen, of some local importance, crawling with a juvenile vigour among the chrysanthemum pots in the drawing room or becoming mixed up with the table legs. This is not due to an excess of alcohol, (as their facilities are very meagre,) but merely a practical and necessary adaptation in order to progress at the game.

'I got quite a shock on entering the drawing room, to see our Lady Mayor, a fat and somewhat dignified spinster, on her knees apparently salaaming to an extremely virile aspidistra. Though some women, especially spinsters, are known to set great store by such phenomena of nature, our mayor is not suffering from an aspidistra-itis. She is merely hot in pursuit of a dark green nail brush which much to her annoyance has been already sighted by the chairman of the local watch committee, whom she dislikes. This crisis however is soon alleviated by the mayor running the brush to ground in the far corner of the eighth leaf north west. But it is followed by a further adverse situation when spurred on by her triumph she attempts to rise with a sudden alacrity which is faster than her normal mobility. Being somewhat like a horse which has gone rather feeble in the legs which requires to scrape and paw the ground before making the actual ascent, she is unable therefore to achieve anything so sudden. She rises, fails nobly in the effort, and crashes to the floor again carrying with her the entire contents of the silver table.

'The result is something bordering on a model arial bombardment, staged by the air ministry for the instructions of students. From every corner of the immediate vicinity silver things are seen hurtling through the air and crashing with a disturbing ferocity on the floor beside the indignant mayor. Our hostess rushes forward in great consternation and attempts to lift her from the floor. Even Mr Everton (the chairman of the local watch committee) is moved by this prostrate position of his adversary and rushes forward to assist also. At first it appears that the task is beyond even their combined efforts and it will need a superhuman strength to achieve success, but after some moments with the help of Mr Malory, the Bank Manager, (who arrived in time to assist at the north-east corner,) the mayor is once more restored to her normal equilibrium. She stands brushing the dust from her frock and laughing in a deep echoing manner to cover her embarrassment.

'Mr Pinhoe, a fat jolly little man, hastily restores the fallen silver ware to the table patting that and the mayor soothingly in turn and getting a little muddled as to which to address his remarks to. 'Never mind,' he says mildly to a silver dish!

'When the whirl of excitement is over the guests who had gathered round, to see the fun, disperse to continue their search. But this exciting episode has somehow cooled their enthusiasm for the game and they

187

wander about aimlessly and begin chatting together in groups.

'Soon after this the hostess standing on the hearth rug ringing a small lunch bell, calls off the hounds and a general adding up of lists ensues. The net result of this labour is that a strange looking man called George with a pedantic voice and red hair has achieved the enormous effort of finding twenty-seven out of thirty-three objects and is awarded the prize. This is a small box done up in orange paper and tied with string which our hostess stands in front of the fire clasping to her ample bosom until George having disentangled himself from the crowd, and making an elegant bow worthy of a count rescues it from her. Then everybody claps and this happy event being over, we all troop into supper in the icy cold labyrinths of the dining room.

'Here we stand about in groups while strange sandwiches are handed round. I say strange because the sandwiches are always filled with things which no one has ever met before. It is really quite amazing how the Pinhoes can do it, but there it is, and it is hardly due to conservatism so much as common sense that none of their guests becomes enthusiastic about them. My next door neighbour Nora Coolhayes is discussing with her brother where she can put her half eaten sandwich this time. The last two years she put it in the flowers and feels now that she ought really to strike fresh ground.

'Mrs Ronaldson her next door neighbour (who is rather sleek and resembles an exclusive Cheshire cat) is pawing the ground like an impatient horse and trying to persuade Humphrey Coolhayes to procure her a whisky and soda to warm her up. Humphrey, who has already had two whiskies and sodas out of the ancient and ancestral butler and feels it may be quite likely he will need another before long, is unwilling to cooperate in this scheme.

'All the other guests are given small tumblers full of an unctious looking red concoction which as Humphrey remarks appears to be principally red ink. This is supposed to be claret cup but its taste is far from that usually attributed to such stuff. It fails entirely to warm the cockles of the heart, or any other part of the anatomy literally or metaphorically. In spite of the overpowering chill in the dining room sleepiness creeps on us and some of the guests begin to yawn and stand silent contemplating the scene.

'However their reveries are suddenly broken by Mrs Ronaldson who returns to the crowd triumphantly carrying a whisky and soda. 'I wished the butler a happy New Year and he gave me one, but I bet he splits to Pa Pinhoe tomorrow morning,' she says with a glint in her eye.

'After the sandwiches the most extraordinary type of pastries are handed round, also with strange fillings. This is followed by trifle, rich and jammy and surmounted by cream which tastes of scalded milk.

'After the repast we adjourn to the hall again where some considerable time is pleasantly passed in playing pass the football. This game is a sort of relay race in two rows one consisting of men and one of women and passing a football over the head and back to the person behind you. George marks himself out as an obvious leader of men by becoming self-appointed captain and urging his side on with yells of 'Come on chaps', 'On your life hurry', 'Keep it steady', 'Look slippy' and similar sportive jargon. Owing to George's profound energy and leadership the men are well up at the end of the round. But we discover later that as they have nobly chosen the position by the bow window (where Mr Mallory later informs us there is an absolutely sizzling draught) we feel this victory is entirely appropriate in order to counteract the definite drawbacks of their position. We on our side have the fire which although hardly of a noticeable quality is at least not a definite drawback.

'As the witching hour of midnight draws on it is suggested that we welcome in the New Year by dancing Sir Roger de Coverley. Every one is quite prepared for this as it is done every year, but welcome the suggestion with a satisfactory display of animated surprise. Every one falls in with the idea and of getting warm through exercise there is a scramble while the assembled company sort themselves into opposite camps. The son of the house, an amiable but rather simple specimen who tries to farm without any apparent success, asks Mrs Shaw, a rather flat-footed old lady married to an elderly squire, to partner him. They head the procession. A somewhat indigent looking gramophone is set in motion. Then consternation ensues among the party for the gramophone record is found to be missing. After an extensive search it is discovered that our hostess (who is extremely fat) has sat down on it and quite irretrievably smashed it to atoms. Being a determined and forceful woman however who is never beaten she suggests sticking it together. It is only with the greatest difficulty that she is restrained from putting this idea into practice by Mrs Ronaldson who explains caustically that even if it would stick together the melody produced would resemble the Lambeth Walk done on a rough Channel crossing.

'This conclusion being arrived at we decide (since there are no volunteer performers for the piano, not even George,) that we must sing the melody ourselves in order to enable us to trip the light fantastic toe. There is some faint indecision at first among the assembled company, but with time a bar or two of music trembles into being while others taking heart fall to and increase the volume. It is not exactly a convincing performance, even George is a little put off by it, and remains hesitant at first but finally takes a strong line in an entirely different key to anybody else. Mrs Shaw who in her youth has held Edwardian drawing rooms spellbound by her singing is determined to stage a come back and trills recklessly in a higher key. These small discrepancies of tune might have been overlooked had everyone been of like mind as to how the music fitted in with the steps. This however seems to cause a good deal of consternation among the company, some of whom have little idea of the dance. A young thing at the end of the line, who has not known the delight of Sir Roger before, leads off half way through the round, instead of at the end. A whole group of people follow her with an insipid young man with a guardsman's moustache who is her partner, running like sheep bolting through a hole in the hedge.

'Down at the other end, however, where the older generation are making a firm stand not to budge till the correct moment, a good opposition is created and the front line troops hold their position strongly. The result is that there is complete chaos for some moments. The young thing stands about vaguely holding up a pair of delicate white arms to form an arch while the young man looks desperately across at her being unable to reach her owing to the extremely solid figure of Mrs Shaw whose behind portion bars the way indomitably. Luckily this complete breakdown of organisation causes such surprise among the persons taking part that each in turn becomes speechless and the dance is brought to a standstill automatically.

'Mrs Pinhoe then takes charge of the situation firmly and suggests that as it is nearly midnight we should sing 'Auld Lang Syne.' We do this with much heartiness urged into such jubilant expression by the thought of the immediate possibility of seeking our own fireside at home, Mr Trafford the barrister and Mr Richardson (both of whom have clung tenaciously to easy chairs by the fading fire rather like men clinging to a life boat in an angry sea) are persuaded at last to relinquish their hold on these and join in the festivities.

'When this is over the ancient butler appears with an attendant satellite and doles out from a basin, whisky punch in small doses, described by Humphry Coolhayes as a mouth wash. In spite of the fact that this beverage appears chiefly made of water it faintly revives the senses as it trickles down, just sufficiently to stimulate the wish in George for more which is not provided however. After this the Pinhoes' nephew, a strange looking young man with long hair who looks as if he comes from a lawyer's office in Bristol, doles out pieces of evergreen wishing everybody a happy New Year. Then someone suddenly discovers by switching on the wireless that the New Year has not come in yet. So he has to stop giving out evergreens and there is a considerable hold up in the whole ceremony for a few minutes until Big Ben has solemnly struck the hour of midnight.

'This evergreen ceremony being over we all adjourn upstairs where there is a touching reunion with our warm coats. Descending to the hall we are met by our hostess who has shouldered a disapproving looking

194

Pomeranian dog under her arm in order to allow it to say goodnight to us. This dog (which has spent the entire evening shut up in an adjourning room downstairs yapping furiously) is naturally not disposed to view us with enthusiasm. In response to polite protestations of admiration from the departing guests it merely returns a watery smile and casts suspicious glances out of the corner of its eye as if about to snap. Saying goodbye to our hostess at a safe distance from its nose, we dash out across the drive to the parking place, not waiting for the car to join the queue at the front door so anxious are we to get to our homely fireside. On the way home we compare notes with each other on our individual experiences and agonies and realise with a certain wonder that we have again safely passed the ordeal of another New Year party at the Pinhoes.'

14

Light Everlasting

One of my most important journeys out to that wider landscape beyond the nursery window was to go with my brother to Yorkshire to stay with the parents of his schoolfriend. It was a great surprise to my mother that I ventured so far because I had hitherto been so afraid of leaving home. Even to go to Nanny's was an adventure. But I had this great desire to equal my brother in everything and when the invitation to stay was made because they had a daughter called Ruth too, I felt that I must get involved in this exploit.

Staying in this old stone manor house in the Yorkshire dales with its very exact and punctual programme was very different to the Vicarage. They gave many things for the local church bazaars, making papier maché bowls out of sugar bags and sewing dainty little things. It was during the latter sessions that an apparent chance event made a link so important to me in the future.

Ruth's mother would read to us aloud; to

me it seemed a fascinating occupation and she happened to choose the story of a past age in a strange northern land called Norway which was hardly known to me then. The book was called *Kristin Lavransdatter* and was by Sigrid Undset.

I was not to realise then how significant this link would be.

Years later after we had made some trips abroad and got more used to the idea of going far from home, my mother started an idea we should go to Norway for a holiday. She always went away very tired and she thought it would be so restful to go on the boat and watch the scenery without any effort. Strangely enough I was loath to go, saying it was very far away and rained a lot. However some much travelled friends were going and so we took heart and accompanied them on a British ship. My preconceived ideas of Norway were quite wrong.

I shall never forget the fascination of seeing the small grey islands with the little winking beacons that heralded the first sight of the coast and then the bright little huts built right down by the sea and lit by brilliant sunshine. Somehow it fascinated me from the very first glimpse and as we travelled on to Balholm and many famous places on the fjords, I became more attracted to it.

Our greatest experience was however when we came again the next year on a Norwegian boat, the *Meteor*, previously the Kaiser's yacht, and went on a cruise right up the coast to the far north and the land of the midnight sun, to Nord Kapp.

I still have in my mind's eye the scene when we stepped out of the barren Customs Shed on the Tyne Commission Quay and saw the *Meteor* standing there, all lit up with her delicate white and gold prow outlined against the dark waters, and music from the ship orchestra was already drifting over the air. It was as if we were sailing into fairyland, and in a sense we were.

I chiefly remember the strange name of the Cape which has stuck in my mind ever since.

I had always thought that inside the Arctic Circle the land was barren and vegetation scarce, but when we had crossed the barrier of that imagined line so familiar to our map-trained minds as to be almost a reality, we saw no sudden change into the barren regions its name suggested. Only the weather became more brilliant, and as we advanced the vegetation grew extensively. The boat stopped at one point to allow us to visit the Svartison Glacier. The woods were alive with flowers, for July is the time of spring so far north. They grew in such a bewildering carpet under the small, bushy trees, that it was almost impossible to take in the varying varieties individually. Most, however, were small in shape, all were exquisitely coloured in pastel blues and pinks, each with a tiny middle picked out in perfect detail. The whole ground was carpeted with lush moss framing each cluster of colour.

When we reached the glacier, we found it a great sheet of white towering above us, with the openings to caves on its edge curving back like the petals of a plant in deepest azure blue. A herd of reindeer came up the valley, strange, woodybrown creatures moving slowly and patiently together, their bells sounding on the air metallically.

Back on our ship, the boat crept onwards up the coast, winding its way through the interminable array of rocks and peaks of the Norwegian coast, now fiercely grey in a raging storm, now lit by the tranquil radiance of the summer sun. We expected to see the midnight sun about two days after this. Meanwhile, each day got longer, the soft glow of perpetual sunset lasted into the night, and sunrise blended with it.

Towards midnight on the second day, we gathered on deck full of expectancy. The weather was good, we might fulfil our great wish, and see the midnight sun. (For it is not every traveller's privilege.) The sun was brilliant overhead, and then, crossing a fjord, we turned into the lee of a huge hill.

The waters were glassy and dark green now in the shadow, giving a vivid impression of their unfathomable depth. The hillside had gone suddenly dark. It towered above us in sinister brooding. Only on the far side the sun broke through by the span of the hill, and fell in a flood of golden light, illuminating with amazing intensity a low-lying strip of green land on which a few houses clustered.

Then, gliding effortlessly on, we turned with that slow and imperceptible grace of movement with which a ship negotiates the intricacies of a fjord, and rounded the rocky barrier running into open water in full view of the sun.

Suddenly, the landscape was lit with a light so glorious, so golden as to be almost beyond comprehension. It seemed as if we had passed from this dreary world into that heaven which has more brilliant pastures than ours to offer.

On the right lay a tiny village nestling on the fjord shore, its houses painted in a glowing red, tinged with the brown of cedar wood. They shone brilliantly now, tiny intense foci of colour on which the light fell dazzlingly. They resembled dolls' houses, too Lilliputian and delicate to house human inhabitants. Around them lay acres of small meadows, ablaze with buttercups, their clear yellow contrasting with the vivid green of the lush grass. Behind these were woods clothed in spring green, not great forests, but small, intimate patches, which mingled with the meadows and stretched upwards to the barren hills that towered behind them.

The sun now visible continued to descend in the sky. Then, at the appropriate moment, a shot rang out from the boat breaking the great stillness. We gazed unbelievingly at the sky. Sure enough, the great golden ball checked its descent, and slowly began to our amazement to climb again into the sky. It seemed incredible to our conventional thought to see a fully visible sun reverse its course, so naturally does the mind imagine sunset as the complete annihilation of the sun itself for a period of time. With steady and almost imperceptible movement, it rose again.

For two days and two nights, it remained like this, knowing no night nor any dimming of the sun, only a vivid golden light transcending everything.

We climbed the circuitous path to the top

of the North Cape, and though it took us two hours, the sun still looked down on us, though we had encountered fog on the fjord below. It shone out of a clear blue sky, and fell on the banks of cloud just below the top of the Cape lighting them so they appeared like acres of pack ice stretching out towards the illimitable distance around the Pole.

A Norwegian, evidently overhearing us speak of our impressions of the scene, ran over the cliff top to our alarm, as if the outlook was really over solid land, and sat on a ledge, poised over the great abyss, laughing at the alarm on our faces. Truly, he was as agile as a mountain goat.

We wandered back to the post office, the only inhabited place where everyone was crowded together. A soprano was attempting to sing Norwegian folk songs in a shrill voice, punctuated by incessant bangs from the postmaster's stamper as it came down ruthlessly on the hundreds of postcards scribbled by the visiting tourists at this unique place in the world. To give it full souvenir value the place must be indelibly stamped on the card. Even the barren terrain of the North Cape had become of souvenir value in these days of modern travel. When this acoustic competition was ended, we descended the mountain once again, among fields of golden globe flowers, and, appropriately enough, forget-me-nots. Then we boarded the boat, and it swung round on its homeward journey.

It was at Tromso that we said goodbye to the midnight sun, as we sped quietly by the sleeping town. We had visited it on the way up, and found it charming. Dimly one could imagine the soft dusk light hanging over the now deserted streets, and the market place by the quay, the orchards full of mysterious shadows, and the flowers strong-scented in the cool air.

The water around the boat was like a vast stretch of shining brown velvet, over which we skimmed, ruckling it into strange folds and curves at the prow, enhancing its beauty, yet never breaking its curved rhythm into spray. The sun, now partly obscured by the hills behind us, shed its light in isolated silver patches on the dark water. Somewhere inshore, where a soft mist was rising, a rowing boat was anchored with dim figures bending and moving in it as they fished patiently through the northern summer night. Suddenly, the light disappeared. We crept forward in a chill and awesome dusk, leaving the sun behind the receding hills to shine on rock and glacier, on sea and land, permeating all with its transcending beauty, an unending glow in the Arctic summer which knows no night.

We were not to know then that this remote and peaceful land that had known a hundred years of peace would be involved in war all through the 'accursed corridor', as it was sometimes known, only five miles long, down which the railway ran conveying iron ore from Sweden to the ice free port of Narvik. The homes that we saw were ravaged and destroyed in the terror of war by the retreating Germans, applying the scorched earth policy.

Yet in spite of the barren state of the land, the refugees that were taken to camps in Scotland by the British Navy, slipped back to Northern Norway long before the Norwegian Government's Reconstruction Programme had established homes for them, so great was the fascination of this strange and wonderful land.

15

Moving to Mysterious Mellbreak

The early part of the war found us in the Lake District waiting for a vacant house at Jordans, where we had decided to settle permanently. An estate rather than a village it had Quaker and international links that were of particular attraction to us, and it was in easy reach of London. But the problem was to find a house there. Meanwhile we were to discover that the Lakes had a peculiar fascination which we would never forget. This was partly because accidentally or perhaps providentially we were to take up our abode on the edge of that mysterious mountain Mellbreak. We stayed at a vegetarian guest-house in Grasmere at first. We were amazed to see in the local newspaper a bungalow advertised to let, at a place called Loweswater. It seemed too good to be true that a place like this was free and being advertised when there was a mass evacuation of both London and Liverpool. Was there some snag about it?

We decided to consult the local artist, Heaton Cooper, at whose studio we had just been admiring his pictures and those his father did of Norway. We felt a special link with him as his mother was Norwegian and the parents had met at Balholm which we had visited on our cruise. When we showed him the advert he was amazed. 'You have just been here and told me you know Balholm where my parents were married and now you come and ask me about Loweswater where I spent my honeymoon. Go over at once and secure it. It belongs to the Happy Ladies, two Quakers who live in a cottage nearby.' So to cut a long story short we did. It was a strange little place made of two army huts from the previous world war, but what a glorious situation.

Since the area of Loweswater is far less known and frequented by the ordinary tourist I am glad to say it is important to explain where it is. There is a chain of three lakes in this area. Buttermere is perhaps the best known, encircled at the top by high mountains. At the other end after a small area of flat land looms Crummock Water and almost on its shores is the village of Loweswater. Here is a fairly large area of fields and houses with the church and inn, the typical attributes of any English village and further on over the brow of a small hill comes the lake of Loweswater.

Turning over some old papers, I came across a record of these days. Its cover was black with the effects of the fire at my house which must have swept over it, yet in some miraculous manner the book escaped destruction and the description of that strange changing valley and its shadowing mountains. I was very glad to find it for although the personalities we knew then remain in my mind, the details of the changing moods of Mellbreak mountain and the fascination of Crummock Water could not be memorised so easily and recreated.

So I have copied its pages so that others may understand and share the pleasure of those wonderful days:

'We arrived after a weary and mundane journey, amid our welter of belongings crammed into the taxi so tightly that we almost seemed to merge into them, being denied any possibility of seeing the view. This was humiliating, for man in his pride does not like to appear as a chattel among things that he normally commands and uses in such superiority. This feeling of being weighed down added also to our physical discomfort and the sensation of anxiety about our safe transportation.

'The tremendous weight of our boxes might cause skidding on the wet roads or would the engine fail on the steep hills? To have got one taxi to bring us on this journey in war-time was surprising enough. However could we find another with sufficient petrol to come and rescue us?

(That the possibility of bombs and destruction in the south should tie us to our worldly goods so much, making us move like a snail carrying its house on its back was yet another example of how war led to the inevitable distortion of normal life.)

'Much to our surprise we arrived safely after all and there was the little hut with its chimney nobly smoking, on the edge of the mountain, doing its best to welcome us.

'The mountain of Mellbreak did not hold out a welcoming hand however, but then that is not her habit. She is a sinister mountain. The rain which had begun at Grasmere was still coming down steadily as if with a relentless purpose. Mellbreak herself was veiled in a cloud which hung down from her pointed summit in two grey strands like a veil shrouding some mysterious oracle. It was as if she was waiting until the proper time to reveal herself to us.

'The other mountains surrounding Crummock Water had disappeared entirely, apparently into higher worlds. The thick opaque clouds which obscured them came right down to the lower slopes. In between, however, where great clefts ran into them, the wind had half opened a path the eyes could follow giving one the impression of a mysterious road leading into infinite space. Leading up to these clefts there were patches of bracken that caught the grey light in some strange way, becoming almost phosphorescent in their gleaming brown.

'Gradually we unloaded all our paraphernalia and took it indoors. When we had paid the taxi man he turned his car round and disappeared into the mist leaving us with a strange feeling of desolation almost being cut off from civilisation on the side of that eerie mountain. But soon 'the Happy Ladies' came to greet us, our kind ladies from the cottage down below, their rosy cheeks and Quaker stability brought courage to our anxious minds. Surely being here was more truly living than our life in the south where it was dominated by the fear of bombs and sophisticated services being cut off like light and heat.

'When we had unpacked all our chattels and settled in chattering rather like a flock of birds settling for the night, complete silence reigned. There was no distant murmur from any main road traffic or a train puffing through the night, only the occasional cry of an owl or a sheep baaing. There was a drowsy idleness about the valley next morning and yet a sense of serene expectancy in it all. It resembled the silence of autumn until one looked closely at the trees and saw the mysterious preparations for spring in the early forming of the buds and the realised miracle of the abundance of spring waiting to come.

'We walked up the lane to the village and asked at the Kirk Stile Inn the way to the paraffin shop. Life was made up here of such simple events and the obtaining of these necessities. They goaded one into action and yet left the brain time to think about other things. The Kirk Stile was never closed; during unlicensed hours it never assumed the severe lifeless facade most pubs do when the bars are shut. For it was also a farm and life must go on there all day. In the yard at the back there was a man with a red face clearing up the deep chocolate-coloured mud the rain had brought there.

'The buildings were whitewashed and in one we saw a group of red calves penned up for the night behind some wooden bars across their door. They were looking out with their limpid eyes motivated by a friendly curiosity about us as strangers. We asked the man about the paraffin shop. 'You follow right

210

round by the church,' he said. They always say 'follow' round here but sometimes it is rather a puzzling direction. This time it proved accurate and we found 'the shop', a tiny white-washed cottage with a large and very clean Clumber Spaniel sitting on the doorstep, rather like one of those ornaments one puts outside a shop to advertise it. Having made friends with the spaniel and the owner of the shop, we made our needs known and got the tin we had brought filled up. If bombs fell and cut off the main electric cables that would not trouble us but the strong smelling stuff in this tin was vital to us. We returned down the lane carrying the can very carefully.

'As we came home, the rooks in the vicarage rookery were settling for the night. There is something dignified about the call of rooks, they have the ring of tradition in them, even in early spring or the drowsiness of summer afternoons. Their call is without the jarring interruptions of historic events in the world. They are wise creatures who know the satisfaction of free speech and are constantly exercising it.

'When we got back it was getting dark so we lit the lamp and gathered round its cheerful glow, not the sharp penetrating light of the electric bulb, but one that fell clearly on the table cloth and objects in its immediate vicinity but left much of the room full of soft mysterious shadows.

'A gale came on that night and the little hut rocked with the force of it driving up the valley, but it remained upright, I am glad to say.

'The atmosphere grew very cold and when we drew the curtains back in the morning, we found brilliant sunshine and all the mountains visible with the tops covered with snow. There is something very arresting about its feathered mantle lying lightly on the higher slopes with seared markings in each crevice crumpling a little but never breaking its fine radiance since no one can step on it. On the lower slopes there was only a skittering of it lying here and there like fine powder on the dark shadowy sides like castor sugar sprinkled over a huge brown cake. The wind in the north was very cold but as our little hut faced directly south we were able to have lunch out of doors sitting in the sun.

'The sky was intensely blue now above the mountains and the air was keen and clear. It seemed utter peace and then suddenly the silence was broken by a hideous cry followed by the baying of hounds not giving tongue like southern hounds but baying fiercely in keeping with the landscape on which they moved. It made one understand the fascination of one's primitive ancestors for the chase but to our more enlightened minds it portrayed only the barbaric dismemberment of an animal grown weak through exhaustion by the chase.

'When they had passed a farmer came by. He had found one of his sheep dead in the corner of the field, killed perhaps by the rigours of the cold at night? Death seemed all round us on this lovely morning. He buried it clumsily. The ground was very hard to dig in, and so went his way.

'Last night it was very cold again and frosty. The moonlight lit up Crummock Water like a vast mirror. Then we heard the purr of enemy planes going over in their hoards to bomb Liverpool, quiet merchants of death flying low creeping along the line of the lakes and probably enjoying the beautiful moonlight scene, forgetting war as we did for no one observed a blackout here. There were not even ordinary curtains you could draw at some people's windows. They seemed to live remote from the idea here and let the light stream forth. Who would want to bomb us they would say? We have no guns here. It was a sort of understood truce and that was why the bombers could fly low and enjoy the beauty of the scene, I suppose. But we knew they carried a load of death for the crowded areas of Liverpool as our own bombers going out through another area of the sky, did on their journey to Hamburg. Oh, the futility of war and men's destruction of one another!

'Dogs came this morning, I don't know why. Perhaps they scented the hounds' recent visit and thought they would see what had been going on. The first were two whippets, slipping easily through the five-barred gate sideways and then stopping to sniff the air alertly. After that they moved on zigging across the field, inspecting the Happy Ladies' house en route, with a mixture of curiosity and nervous hesitancy. Then they passed out of sight by one of the hedgerows, drawing it for rabbits no doubt before they returned home.

'Then came the fat curly-coated dog from the village; he had bits of brown on him making him look like a miniature airedale. He moved in a slow, leisurely fashion like the village folk he lived among. He sniffed the morning air sometimes as if he found it interesting and then went down to the field in front of the cottage where Jock the Scotch Terrier lived, who joined him, barking at first indignantly. It was a sort of forced annoyance to protect his territory because his tail was wagging at each bark as if he was really quite pleased to have the advantage of a visitor in his quiet life. Finally he capitulated and calmed down inspecting his visitor in detail and with great curiosity.

'After this came Peggy the Cairn. She lives at the farm where five lanes meet. When you pass she smiles at you and shows her teeth alternately and then runs on ahead looking back to ask if you will go for a walk with her.

'Like many bitches she is rather shy by nature and today she came down with great hesitancy and her tail hanging down and between her legs. She was like an only child who does not seem quite sure she should join in when others play.

'Soon they were all gone on their various doggy errands and no one would know there had been this strange mass movement over very interesting terrain to satisfy doggy curiosity.

'Today we had to fetch the bread from Miss Becks, another of those domestic duties connected with essential supplies that forces one into action here.

'These two sisters live in a cottage on the 'main' road from the village, if you could call it main. It is on a slope just below the vicarage, and the cottage a very old one,

215

nestles into the hillside conveniently taking shelter from it. Inside the sisters waited to greet us, one fair, one dark. It was the darker one who seemed to take the initiative. She had a strange dignity about her and though she was not beautiful to look at there was a personality about her that you could not help but feel. Her dark eyes had a depth in them.

'The family had lived there for years and their roots were very firm like the cottage. Nothing had been done to alter it. She showed us with pride how the oven built at the side of the present range was the original one and ideal for baking bread.

'Certainly the results were very good as we found after walking home clasping two warm crusty loaves in our arms we sat down to eat them generously spread with butter from the local farm. There was not much left of one loaf after the meal and as we relaxed in the strange medley of 'easy' chairs provided in the hut we felt indeed that bread is the staff of life.'

★ ★ ★

You could not know Loweswater without knowing Charles. He was the great personality of the village. He lived at the pub, technically serving behind the bar but with great adaptability he would cross the narrow road between the two and serve at the altar in the church with equal alacrity, in fact one wondered if he got his duties sometimes confused in his mind. He was plump and red in complexion rather like a Toby jug and endowed with something of the same jolly appearance and wit.

I recall this on one occasion when the vicar insisted on lending my mother his long clerical cloak because it was raining when they came out of early church. When my mother returned it she gave it to Charles to put back in the vestry, explaining that the vicar had lent it to her. Charles exclaiming loudly at this kindness, added in a hushed whisper 'Oh I wish I had seen you in it, you must have looked just like King Charles!'

We often pondered on why King Charles? My mother had never been likened to that monarch before.

Charles's efforts were not always motivated by common sense and sometimes got a little out of hand, as one story from the past portrayed.

There was on Mellbreak the lair of a rare bird, the Peregrine Falcon. It lived with its young in a small cave in the rocks on the steepest part of the mountain. Some young men decided they would do an article on these birds for *Country Life*. But how to observe them, that was the question. I knew from personal experience these birds are unerring in perceiving your presence. Even when I hid behind a wall a mother bird returning to the nest would see me, and in some mysterious way, without a sound as a warning, the terrible clamour from her young, which was as noisy as a whole school yard at play, would suddenly be changed into utter silence. How did she do it?

Well, the young men wanted to do something to offset this, no doubt, so they hit on the idea of building an eyrie up against the rock but covered by trees. They somehow got some timber and were working out a splendid plan. But the hut was occupied by a nervous lady at that time, who had just come home from being a missionary in war-ridden China.

Although no war had started in Europe then, she decided that the Germans had landed already and were putting guns into the mountain side. She ran frantically to the village to summon help where of course she came across Charles who reacted rapidly to her dramatic story. Never staying to question its authenticity he roused the village and by some extraordinary power, collected a sort of private militia. Armed with the few guns they could muster and sticks and stones, they set out to rout the enemy and retake their beloved Mellbreak again.

Imagine the embarrassment and frustration of the two young men seeking to hide themselves away quietly from the birds when this apparent rabble besieged them defeating all hope of photos or observations for their article, at any rate that day. How they managed to make their true identity known was never explained, but no doubt their very Englishness soon laid the lie and the would-be 'militia' returned quietly to their own homes and more domestic activities leaving the mountain to its traditional peace. For although they lived among those glorious heights few local people ever went near them other than a shepherd looking for a sheep or some other practical reason. Ramblers came from afar and walked on them and this caused no comment they were 'foreigners' and liked to do this sort of thing, but when someone local did it merely to take exercise or see the view that was considered most odd.

My mother and I therefore were not aware how much we were circumventing local tradition when we climbed Mellbreak. Having lived for some time under its shadow it seemed to us only natural that we felt an urge to know it from above too.

Had we been mountaineers and chosen to make a perilous journey up the steep rocky face of it, it would not have caused any local comment I expect. Mountaineers were foreigners who did this sort of thing, not even a group of ramblers, for those were people who pass by, but for a self-respecting resident of the village, a mother and daughter who would normally be associated with carrying out domestic duties at a much lower level, to do this ascent was something quite out of the ordinary and met with the disapproval of the locals; perhaps subconsciously they even felt challenged by this 'feat'.

Actually, climbing Mellbreak was quite an easy task really if you knew how. We discovered that you could walk up it at the back by a series of comparatively small rises by a wide open area like a broad footpath which avoided the slippery path which marked the mountain in its steeper sides, and this mostly gave you short turf beneath the feet.

When we reached the top we lay down on it and thanked God we had done it. I don't recall feeling any particular thrill at having achieved this 'climb'. Perhaps it was because no one would praise us for achieving the impossible; it was all too long, almost like an urban walk. There was a wonderful view from the top. What is there in height which instills one with awe?

But apart from this I felt that the real heart of Mellbreak lay in her steeper part as if that 'face' that we looked up to from the hut was where the great centre the mysterious personality or presence of the mountain lay hidden.

It was some days later, having tea with our neighbour, Mrs Bell, that we realised the atmosphere of disapproval associated with our exploit. The Bells lived in what had been a small farm, up a lane rather than a drive you could call it, marked by a stone wall on both sides. Mr Bell had long ago become too crippled with rheumatism to do anything active on the place, but they had doubtless saved a bit in their working life and that and the pension gave them enough for the modest needs of their two selves and the dog, a small kind of sheepdog-cum-Lakeland terrier which shared their home but not their menu, for we were rather disturbed to hear that it was fed chiefly on potatoes.

Mrs Bell was a very striking-looking old lady with that natural beauty and dignity that is often found among country folk. She had beautiful features and a fine complexion with natural colour in it resulting, I presume, from the fine mountain air. To give as it were a perfect background to this she had lovely white hair which was naturally wavy, drawn back from her temples by hair combs, and coiled up into a bun on top of her head, a perfect balance to her fine features.

Tea, of course, was a proper meal in Loweswater, not just a pot of tea with a grocer's cake hastily torn from its cellophane container. There were home made scones and jam, and of course several sorts of cake, which Mrs Bell had produced with her own hands.

These were eaten in a leisurely fashion with some considerable conversation in between like the filling in a sandwich.

I cannot recall now what we talked about; had we been local no doubt it would have been mainly gossip about local people but as we knew few this was not possible. I think as a whole we compared our differing ways of life in the north and south, differences that were accepted without any comment or surprise.

It was when we touched on life in the local sphere and mentioned our climbing of Mellbreak that things came alive. Mrs Bell thought of it as an incredible thing for my mother to have done and stated emphatically that she had never been to the top and one felt that she did not wish to either, so strong was the note of disapproval in her voice. In fact the subject was quickly passed over and the conversation changed as if we had mentioned something bordering on immorality.

Our other immediate neighbours were the widow of a parson from a nearby parish and her daughter. They were rather reclusive and seldom went out. Shopping was probably something of a rarity for them because they claimed to be so self-supporting. They had never throughout the war used a coupon. The thick worsted skirts they wore, in fact most of their clothes, were made out of the bits of wool that sheep left on the hedgerows when they squeezed through a gap or scraped their backs on barbed wire. These small often dirty bits they collected, combed, washed and spun and then made up into these wonderful tweed garments. I can't recall that we ever called on them which seems rather unneighbourly when I look back, but there seemed to be some unwritten law locally that you did not disturb their privacy. The only expedition they seemed to make was out to church on Sunday mornings and they generally sat behind us and the mother showed no shyness now or wish to remain unnoticed, for she sang very loud and much too high; in fact I thought entirely out of tune, but a farmer's wife who became our friend was most impressed by it. 'Eie,' she said to us one day after church, 'did you hear Mrs — Didn't she pipe up loovely?'

Truly, what is one man's meat is another man's poison.

Individual choral efforts were rather remarkable in that church. There was the evacuee lady who brought her children with her and her old mother. The latter wore a hat which much resembled that of Napoleon. She had a lantern jaw in which the lower one was as hard and definite as if it was made of stone. When we sang 'Onward Christian Soldiers, marching as to war,' her enthusiasm knew no bounds and I shall never forget her profile, for some reason she stood rather sideways in her pew outlining her large tricorn hat and her square jaw working up and down as if it was operated by some mechanical aid or the hungry jaws of a crocodile.

The parishioners were all rather backward at coming forward in that it seemed a sort of local etiquette that no one sat in the two front rows of pews. The vicar, however, did not seem disturbed by this at all and we noticed that he often directed his sermons at the empty front pews. When later we became great friends of him and his wife, we asked him about this, he told us he was psychic and quite often saw past parishioners who had died, sitting in them listening to him.

★ ★ ★

'We went out for a walk today all in a hurry for one has to seize on the opportunities here when nature is right for it, and she knows no time table. Looking over towards Loweswater and the pastoral country surrounding it the area was diffused with a golden light which was in keeping with their peaceful beauty, but looking the other way up the valley at the end of Crummock Water where the mountains are stern and heavy, the sun had already gone and had left them dark and lowering, except for a tiny patch of gold which broke through the clouds surprisingly on the other side of the shore, and shone with incredible radiance amid such dark surroundings.

'We walked down to the shore of Crummock Water; the water was deep blue and cold, and whipped up like an angry sea by the bitter wind coming down the valley from Buttermere. It ran up the little beach at our end in small waves and there was the incessant sound of tumbling water and shifting pebbles like the incoming tide makes at the sea.

'From the shore we walked towards Mellbreak and near the fell we saw the body of a poor sheep that had been worried by something. It lay against a stone wall with its head thrown back and its teeth clenched as if it had died there, trapped and in agony. Why must nature be so cruel and why such a sight invade our peace on such an evening walk? Oh for the day when the lion shall lie down with the lamb, but that will not come till 'the earth is full of the Knowledge of the Lord' and how can that be while man is still killing and eating the lamb himself?

'Today we went for a walk up into the mysterious oak wood that lies on the side of Mellbreak. The ground is covered with moss of a dozen different kinds which seems to extend like some huge sheet of green over the lower mountainside. The mosses are all mixed together but it is only when you look closely that you can see the amazing details of them. Some are soft and short and bright green and others tall and spiky and a darker colour, standing up almost like miniature fir trees.

'Even the trunks of trees are covered with something of a sparse woody kind, lichen I suppose you call it. There is something strange about this wood with its sturdy, stunted trees windblown with the gales of perhaps hundreds of years. Oaks do not easily give way. The lichen on the trunks and the sharp angles of the leafless branches remind one rather of an old derelict house. The cart track by the wood bounded by a stone wall was ankle deep in leaf mould from the trees left from last autumn, or perhaps many autumns, it had drifted there like snow.

'We passed a lot of sheep in the wood. Some were the gentle looking white kind, but the others were darker, though not black, and had horns and they looked at us quizzically with rather wicked little eyes of deep amber. When we had climbed out of the wood we took a path to the fell and turned up a cleft in the mountain. The cloud was drifting there, it was like a different world with snow in odd patches and a bitter wind coming towards us so we did not go very far.

'Today it snowed very hard, a blinding blizzard coming down the valley from Scale Hill the opposite way to Crummock Water. This was surprising as it would appear that that valley is full of pastoral country and is pleasant to look at in fine weather, but as it runs north, that is the reason for the origin of such a tempest. The storm swept down relentlessly with that eerie ferocity like it does over the glaciers of Norway. It went on for many hours and our feet felt frozen and the hut seemed to be full of chilly draughts which we attempted to stop.

'About two o'clock when we were busy reading and had forgotten about the outside world we looked up and saw it had cleared and the sun was shining, an amazing transformation. We went for a walk towards Scale Hill and saw all the beauty of a brilliant day. The lower hills were lit by a dazzling golden light, while the spaces below took on a dim blue look, vague and indefinite a perfect foreground for the clear beauty of the hills above.

'We saw a field in the lowlands full of lambs, small bundles of woolly whiteness sitting together in groups and flapping their long ears. They became inquisitive and full of surprise when we looked at them. Next we came to a tiny white farm with grey stone cowsheds hitched on to its side. There was a stream near with a little stone bridge leading up to the farm. A brown horse stood by the house as if to enhance the colour scheme. There was a large hole in the barn roof as if they had not bothered to mend it since the snow fetched the tiles off last year. The farms round here are in poor repair; I suppose the land is too sparse to allow much luxury as one may see on the farms in Shropshire. When walking you often come across some ruined house once a prosperous farm. This is a reminder that those better days are gone and agriculture become the Cinderella of British industry.

'In the valley we saw four gigantic buzzards, their hungry eyes obviously poised for prey. There is something exhilarating but terrifying about their gigantic wing span, the feathery scoop of those great flapping arms and yet it fascinated me to watch their swooping and manoeuvring, a sort of nature's bomber looking for a target, and then when they are tired of looking for their prey, they swoop with an amazing ease over the far mountain and disappear from view.

'We turned homeward and came back up our little lane. We passed a tiny house built somewhat up on a knoll, coloured grey and very prim. Under the one tree in the garden was a little white seat in Victorian style for some figure to sit on but it was empty.

'As we turned the corner in our lane we came to that most perfect of views down Crummock Water to the distant hills beyond. It is strange how the casual eruptive pressures of the ice age which is said to have fashioned this terrain, created such a wonderful panorama as if it had been painted with an artist's brush. What human architect or sculptor could have moved these great blocks of earth and stone and placed them in such perfect symmetry. Surely there must be a creative mind behind it all?

'In fact when you stand at our end of Crummock Water in an evening after snow and see the way its deep blue waters bend into the girdle of the mountains at the end giving a feeling that it goes on into eternity, it is easy to think that all this is still in its primitive state and the ice age has only just left the land.

'There was an amazing stillness about Crummock Water tonight making it seem like a forgotten world, its surface looking almost solid in its immaculate smoothness. The boat house on the other side looked like a tiny cardboard toy. Even the white farm over the water was strangely unreal, as if it was, part of a world left empty of humans, an inanimate memory.

'The mountain slopes look steep and rather cruel so black are their rocks against the snow. The cloud came drifting relentlessly down on the summit like some great area of depression after the warm sunshine and icy patches of snow below stood out crudely.

'But as I leant on the balcony I heard the evening chorus of the birds echoing up and down the valley from the sparse trees, in it, the clear notes of a thrush, so living and radiant. The warning note of a blackbird who detected a predator — and then the cry of a lamb, and the world seemed to be alive again.

'I wonder if the mountains talk together. It seemed as I stood on the balcony later in the gathering dusk as if they must be speaking in a low majestic sort of way but, talking in a manner as little comprehensible to us as the affairs of State would be to a child, then silence seemed to surge round, and a strange emptiness that seemed to press on the ear drums until the bark of a dog would have been a God-sent release. Suddenly one was filled with an urge to send a sudden cry forth, travelling on this boundless emptiness of the universe. Perhaps that is what inspired Munch's picture The Shriek?

'Then suddenly sound was restored and the silence broken as an owl cried, sad and eerie on its evening hunt in the sodden marshes below. Not a soul answered it; only clouds moved slightly on the mountain's face, lifted like the veils of a mourner in a breeze and then sank down again in their grey emptiness, and the night crept down.

★ ★ ★

'It rained today rained and rained again and the clouds covered the mountains so completely that only a narrow strip of the lower slopes in the valley could be seen at all.

'Then suddenly the sky lightened and they rolled back, slowly and gently revealing each field and fell as if it was a new world just created, a panorama unseen by man before. The soft turf still running with water gave off the smell of damp earth and the coloured patterns of the fell were clean washed and gleaming. A sigh of gratefulness seemed to run through the earth and spring seemed a step nearer.

'The tits got busy in the hedgerows creeping up the leafless twigs so that their blue radiance was half hidden by the intricacies of the grey branches and one was not aware at first of their presence.

'The curlew and the peewit began calling in the marshes, soft ringing cries which seemed to have appropriately something of the liquid notes of water in them and the vast loneliness of the marshy lands they inhabitated. There is nothing more lovely than the clear whistle of the curlew as it spirals down into the grass by Crummock Water. All were preparing for the spring that must forever come again.

'I saw the old white horse down by the stream who stood with his friend the rich lady's horse, they stood together where the rushes are a rich brown and the trees are tinged with gold and they seemed a perfect foil to the field down by the beck.

'In the farmyard too what perfect colours Providence has chosen for the fowls. There the background is white buildings and the dark brown of mud mingled with straw, and then suddenly the fowls make a mock invasion of the farmyard in pursuit of rumoured food. They line out led by a huge game cock with gorgeous feathers, rich coloured Rhode Islands, one clear white hen that stood out against the mud and tiny branches, followed by some with golden feathers which toned in with the shades of moss on the rooftops on the cow sheds.

'We bought some carrots, beetroots and potatoes at the farm and all for 11d! He was a nice boy who served us and he sorted them out so carefully giving us the best. We wondered what he did with himself in these lonely parts in the winter. 'It rains a great deal here, doesn't it?' I said.

' 'Oh I don't know,' he replied. 'Sometimes it does not rain enough.' He laughed in a kindly way but then the conversation ended. He seemed contented enough.

'As we walked back it started to rain again and the first wraith of cloud was coming down on the mountain again creeping ever so stealthily round the sphere of the hill like a cat stalking a mouse. The mountain seemed waiting for the inevitable shrouding of colours on the fell which were overwhelmed with grey oblivion.

'It has rained again today but there have been sudden intervals when the clouds have broken and shed patches of brilliant sunshine on the fields above Crummock Water. The soft yellow grass and the brown bracken stood out suddenly and every grey stone across the valley gleamed wiped clean like a slab with the refreshing rain.

'The clouds have been racing across the mountain at an incredible speed until it almost appeared as if the great mountain itself was moving and might fall on us, and then there was a strange wind in the valley, the sound blending with the noise of the full river and the surging waterfalls like one great volume of the music of nature.

'The foresters lit a fire in the clearing and fingers of blue smoke went swirling upwards and the scent of burnt wood came over the air. The paths over the fields stretched like fingers in the gleaming grass, and it must have been a great day to be walking up there facing the sun and the soft rain on one's face with the music of nature in your ears.

'The rain has gone suddenly tonight and there are such vivid colours in the glen. The farm across Crummock Water never looked so white. It seemed quite dazzling outlined against the twiggy branches of the leafless trees behind it.

'We went out this morning early. The valley towards Buttermere was dark and obscured by the storm but suddenly through it a small open space came in the clouds and a direct spiral ray of sunshine pointed downwards on to the water. This seemed strange for any rays I have previously seen are directed outwards fanwise involving a large expanse of sky. The light was shaped like a search light but it was pointed down to earth to enrich it by the sun not as a search light does, upwards to aid in destruction. As the rays travelled over the grey waters it lit them with patches of gleaming silver and then travelled on to the mountains where they lit the snow with a curious unreal light, phosphorescent, more like a show at the cinema than a freak of nature.

★ ★ ★

'Today has displayed even stranger patterns of light. The hills round us were covered with smoking black cloud drifting across them quickly but down in the valley the sun broke through in patches quite suddenly giving a strange piebald look to the valley. The trees grouped together had a brown feathery look making them appear soft and dim like an old painting.

'The amazing thing about the weather here is its localness, the segregation into different areas. It seemed as if we were in between half a dozen sorts of weather. Over towards Loweswater one could see the fury of the storm making the sky an ominous grey shade, rather like paint-water used to become when as a child one upset it by accident on the table cloth. The mountain itself was utterly black, and only when you looked very hard could you see the faint brown patches that denoted the autumn bracken was still there on Mellbreak's side. Just a little further up the valley the lower more pastoral hills were enjoying the peaceful glow of a pale sunset. Crummock Water was almost completely in darkness while just across it on the other side of the water, where the clouds had broken, there was a strange luminous light which outlined everything in a soft pink shade. The mountains behind this were becoming covered by soft white clouds that came over in batches and having hit the peak suddenly divided into strands like a lady's chiffon scarf tending to creep downwards instead of across.

'When we looked upwards we realised the clouds were doing extraordinary things, one group coming from the mountain straight across while another was coming up the stream and still keeping on persistently. They were crossing and recrossing, the whole thing was like a graceful ballet danced in the sky.

★ ★ ★

'Today when we looked out the mountain towards Scale Hill was dark and rocky and the snow on it lay in sharp white strands making the whole thing resemble a Japanese mountain on some painted fabric.

'Mellbreak looked like some great hippopotamus with leather looking sides and its head resting on its paws. In the oak wood on its slopes the lichen covered trunks shone white and twisted like the grotesque illustrations of Arthur Rackham in *Children's Fairy Stories*. It was all so still this evening and so ominous somehow. The only things that seemed to exist were the thrushes calling from the valley.

★ ★ ★

'*April 4th*. Today was like autumn in its stillness, it was as if everything was tired after the storms, and the air was so soft it made you feel drowsy.

'We went for a walk along the fell towards Buttermere. It was very wet under foot because of hundreds of little streams that were running down from the mountain side. Some of them were hidden by a carpet of green moss and you stepped squelch into them up to the ankles.

'The lake was very quiet and grey today but in the stillness you could hear the gentle lapping of the water on the shore. In its continuity it seemed almost hypnotic. There is something very healing about the sound of running water.

'As we walked on the fell we came across a delightful bird who kept perching on a block of stone, singing and then flying on to another yet never leaving his immediate territory. His feathers appeared to be all of soft cream tones but when he flew his body was clear white under his wings. He sang with the sweetness of a canary and trilled exotically, filling the air with delicate and beautiful notes.

'Round the corner further towards Butter-mere we came to the Gannet Stone, a big rock going up sharply from the shore. On it sat the gannet himself. He always seemed to be in residence. He looked so wise and yet quaint sitting up on that high perch. He appeared rather like a small black penguin at first, but as one got nearer you could see his long neck and beak. He sat very upright just like a dog sitting on his haunches, and he kept looking round out of the corner of his eye as if he felt that there was someone about. We got quite near to him but a little bird with a perky tail hurried away on the wing making a noise like clattering stones, and the gannet flew off into the water, at first circling round with his long neck circled like a swan and then finally taking to flight, and swooping away, spreading out his great wings to their huge span.

'We went further and rounded another corner. We saw a pair of puffins fly out of the water. Such quaint woolly little birds and it was so surprising to see them so far inland. We sat down to watch the lapping waves and as we did so we heard a weird and plaintive cry. A huge white bird like one of the swans in Hans Andersen's fairy story flew overhead with neck outstretched and his great wings covering a vast space. He landed at the other end of the lake.

'We went out the other evening quite late. The mountains were cold and dark and the water the shade of dark grey, the whole picture was one of austerity, but at the side the mountains there were tinges of warm pink which were growing pinker every moment. They lay on the side of an angry grey cloud which we get so much of here, and gradually the pink suffused it until it appeared like a gorgeous shot silk curtain. To the left where the pastoral country lies we saw the smaller hill backed by tiny benevolent clouds, like puffs of smoke, and tinged with the delicate shades of a budding rose so delicate and so varied were they in shade.

★ ★ ★

'Today we walked down to the lake a new way, the sun was shining and everything was particularly radiant in the morning light. We walked under the arch of trees which grew right down to the water's edge, their roots looking so odd and claw-like where there was no soil to cover them and they just clung on to the swamp. They resembled the big roots of seaweed which you find flung up on the beach after a fierce storm.

'There was a chaffinch singing in one of the trees. That to me will always symbolise spring. It reminds me of a wood we used always to visit at home whenever cherry blossom time came and we sometimes found some cowslips in the field on the way there.

'We discovered from this point quite a new angle for the view up Crummock Water. The fact that you could not see it all from here because it bends round, gives it an air of mystery as if it goes on and on, it gives one the impression of vastness that the fjords have in Norway. How this makes one long to be back there. What is the magic that these lovely mountains here don't possess? Is it the vast mountain area and the glaciers among them, or is it as a Norwegian friend believes that they contain a stalagmite connected with the Archangels? I wonder if I shall ever see that country again, or always have to go on apologising for my enthusiasm for explaining its beauty to people who have never seen it and cannot therefore understand.

'I often wonder if the Vikings came here and christened Crummock Water because Krummer means to bend in Norwegian and that is exactly what this lake does. They had left their traces in so many other places in

241

the Lakes. Grisedale, for instance. The Dale of the Pigs for they not only came as raiders but some of them settled as farmers here.

'The birds by the lake are very interesting and somewhat puzzling to identify since I am not an ornithologist. We saw one bird that looked entirely grey until it opened its wings and flew. Then I realised its body was pure white and its very sharp wings which were like a swallow's had a white edge to them on the inner rim. It flew very like a swallow skimming over the water and alighting on stone further on uttering a 'cheep cheep' sound.

'Perhaps it was the same breed of bird that we saw later which was buff brown on top but rather dirty underneath. Was one the cock and one the hen? The strange thing was that although it had a long beak and one would think of the sandpiper family it stood on a tree stump by the lake and ran its beak right into it like a woodpecker. It had quick movements and uttered a sharp shrill cry as it went from one branch on to another.

'Later we saw a brown and white bird walking along the shore, picking up bits as one would expect of this type. When it flew out with a shriek and spread its wings the white rim at the edge showed up as a most distinct V.

'Then three of them foregathered and had a most exciting chase over the lake shrieking and turning, evidently two cocks chasing a hen. After this they moved into some bushes on the lake shore near to us, they appeared to be darting in and out without actually perching on the bushes, yet they seemed to cover very little distance. In fact for a brief space of time it would appear that they were actually hovering and when they did this they arched their wings in the way that angels are portrayed as doing in famous pictures. The extraordinary thing was that the wings moved so quickly when they were hovering that the wings became quite invisible. I sent a description of these birds to the local ornithological society but they could not identify them as a particular breed of sandpiper or kindred bird. The white V on the back so distinctive seemed so specially puzzling that they were difficult to identify, and the fact that they did not keep to the shore entirely like sandpipers do but devoured wood and frequented bushes was even more strange.

★ ★ ★

'The sheep have been causing us great concern. We have had the most torrential rain here for twenty-four hours. The wind was so strong it was almost impossible to stand upright, and the rain blinding like a thunderstorm brings but it kept on and on for hours.

'This weather was terribly hard on the lambs many of whom were only a few days old. They crowded together under the walls, some of them on the leeward side were well sheltered but in many cases the mothers happened to be on the windward side and the lambs with them of course. Poor little things, what a world to be born into.

'The lambs are interesting creatures, some are the traditional type, all white and fluffy but the others though they have white bodies have little black woolly legs as if they were encased in stockings. They have black faces too, but on their knees and cheeks they have a blending of the two colours, a kind of grey effect which looks rather like an oppossum's fur. They have funny little amber eyes which peer out at you arrestingly.

'Two of them we have got to know seem to have rather flippant mothers who go wandering about all over the place and when you enter the field they rush towards you opening their pink little mouths in loud 'barring' as if in protest regarding some recent escapade of their careless parents.

'The others that have good mothers, run to them instinctively for shelter as you approach. I had no idea till I got to know them how the ewes differ in character. We found a genuinely lost lamb and put it back near what turned out to be the right mother and oh what a touching reunion there was.

'We saw a lamb in the kitchen at the Kirk Stile which had nearly drowned in a gulley beside the beck. It had been given whisky and was curled round wrapped in flannel, batting its big ears in contentment.

'When will men cease to kill and eat these exquisite creatures. By an irony this year there may be less slaughtered because so many people are called up for the slaughter of men.

'They told us they lost 20 sheep in the snow. They often live for three weeks, but they were in a gully, the boy got a stick but found it was too deep for him to dig down single handed so they just left them to drown. Why can't people co-operate in a rescue effort? What strange inhumanity to harden their hearts against — this trapped animal life which deserves love and concern.

'The Bible picture of the shepherd makes him such a compassionate figure. The sheep hear his voice and follow him. Here they run away and are rounded up by barking dogs.

If you meet the sheep in the road they are so full of terror that they jump over the wall and the dogs go and hurl them back. They often get stuck halfway and the dogs scare them over into the road again, such a steep drop.

'We saw three generations of dogs. The very old one, a bag of bones, only making an occasional sally at the sheep, barking and then sitting down thankfully, trying to show he was still active in spite of his age.

'There was one very trained and capable one and the young puppy still at the leggy stage, and terribly thrilled at being taken out with the flock and trying so hard to do the right thing, taking a bite at a sheep here and there and then hanging back when the others did, waiting for the next move by them. The sheep dogs have very nice natures really and are clever at rounding up sheep in a proper area like Sheepdog Trials but here they seem to be used so indiscriminately to frighten and chivvy.

'This is partly because the men are so rough with the sheep it creates that sort of atmosphere. We saw them drag sheep by their horns right across the field. Others they caught up suddenly by bits of their backs and flung them over the wall into the next field. It was extraordinary that they did not have

246

broken limbs as a result.

'Sheep seem to suffer from the brutality of countrymen and the stupidity of urban ones for by Crummock Water there is a notice stating it is the water supply for a famous town nearby so no one must bathe there. To safeguard the water's purity the town council had put a steep cement parapet along the lower part of the stream that leads into it. The concrete comes some way up the field. Above this there is still a natural beach for the animals to go down and drink. This is essential. Urban minds had not realised that sheep used to walking in the Beck would stroll down it as far as the concrete area and be unable to get up and out of the stream there, their wool becoming heavy with water they would miserably drown and their bodies were left there unnoticed. I always wondered why the town people did not get typhoid from this contamination. No one seemed to bother about it and remove the bodies.

'Perhaps they did get some form of stomach upset and like most cases of contamination of food, it got put down under that convenient label, gastric flu, or 'something that is going about'.

'In spite of the fact that life is so hard on the sheep and even mother love is not as essential a characteristic as it is in cats with their kittens there is a sort of pattern of life customary habits which bind the breed together. For instance, I wonder what is it that makes lambs form up for what we would call organised games when the witching hour of night is approaching?

'It is wonderful on a summer evening to watch them line up quite voluntarily, very often on the highest point of the field, like children preparing for school sports, and then sprint across the field in a team. What fun they seem to have but what is it gives them this unified elation at that particular time?

'On one occasion I witnessed an individual drama within a little family circle. I was hiding behind a wall so that none of them had any idea I was there.

'The Mother Ewe was sitting by a curious round knoll of stone watching her two lambs gambol and occasionally joining in.

'Father Ram was sitting a little way from them chewing the cud and apparently quietly ruminating on things. Mother obviously made up her mind that he ought to join in the family gambol. She kept looking at him searchingly but he sitting sideways to her, apparently did not see. But somehow the powerful pressure of her thought and her gaze penetrated his protected area. Though he pretended not to see it was plain that he did realise, out of the corner of his eye, what was going on. She just went on staring at him confident eventually it would bear fruit.

'Then suddenly he shrugged his shoulders as it were, got up and playfully charged the children and butted them with his horns.

'They were delighted at Father joining, and ran round and round this odd stone edifice, jumping on and off it, and bouncing with delight as Father made mock sallies at them and they jumped up and out of his way.

'Truly there was a family relationship, a subtle kind of understanding, and contact through thought and visual pressure just like a human family.'

★ ★ ★

As the month of May sped on we realised that if a house did not come up for us at Jordans we should have to leave the Hut as it was let in June every year to a family from the coast who came to spend their annual holiday there.

After a lot of enquiries, for people were not keen to let rooms in their houses, we found a large farm house on the other side of the village near Loweswater Lake where the farmer's wife would kindly take us in. She was to become a great friend of ours.

It was a most remarkable house called High Cross. How it got its name, which seemed an ancient one, I could never find out. You approached it by a fine avenue of trees leading up to a pair of lovely wrought-iron gates between two imposing stone gate-posts which gave it an air of great dignity. The strange thing was that these only marked the entrance to the kitchen garden, not the house. That stood at the left of the avenue, the front door opening on to a tiny garden with only a footpath from the door straight into the field through a small gate. The present house at the front was early Victorian. Had there been some ancient mansion before this to which this dignified avenue and its gates led up?

Certainly the back of the house was very old, but built long before avenues and wrought-iron gates came in. The kitchen showed clearly that originally the fireplace had been in the middle of the floor for the marks were still there from the smoke and the hole had been so clumsily covered over that you could see its outline still on the ceiling.

The heavy wooden doors were so ancient that they had evidently been made before sophisticated tools and nails came in. It was a pity that the wooden screens, which are usually erected by the door to keep the draught from it blowing the smoke from the open fire into the room, had been removed at some time.

Did some Viking found the farm as one of the many early settlements that they built up in that area, often leaving place names like Grisedale (i.e. the Dale of the Pigs) as clues to their activities or even in the language for the local inhabitants still speak of going *til* market as they do in Norway.

I once had a strange dream about the back of the house, the now muddy farmyard was covered with grass. I did not know till I came to re-read *Kristin Laverensdatter* and go to the Folk Museum in Lillehammer that the Vikings' farms always had green turf over the yard round which the house was built, like a 'quad' at a University College does.

As we had moved to the other side of the village, we went more often now to Loweswater rather than Crummock Water, and though it was much less dramatic we came to love its pastoral type of beauty almost as much.

The lower slopes of the hill on the far side of Loweswater from the farm, were planted with larches too, a forestry project on which they were actually working. Quite a lot of girl foresters joined the team, being allotted that as part of their war work.

One girl, however, must have been sensitive to the glorious smell that the fine trees emitted. She fell fast asleep at her work and as it was impossible to wake her, an ambulance was called and she was taken to hospital. There they could find nothing wrong with her, but she continued to sleep for several days until the effects of things had worn off. As far as I can recall she did resume work so perhaps she became tolerant to it. Allergies were not taken so seriously in those days.

Loweswater stretched away into lower country at the far end. This consisted of cultivated fields which ultimately reached down to the coast. When the soft evening light fell on this landscape with its small trees and undulations it looked like an old fashioned print in all its exquisite detail and pastoral beauty.

As it ran towards the west, we used to watch beautiful sunsets light up the horizon on summer evenings.

One night just before Whitsun I had one of my strange precognition dreams from which I woke up saying, 'Stukas will do it.' I had no idea what Stukas were nor what they would do. I only learnt lately that they were a kind of plane which the Germans were using at that time.

On the Saturday night which was Whitsun Eve, we sat out by the lake rather later than usual. The sun had disappeared into a solid grey sky, there had been only a little pink glow that night and we thought that it had gone below the horizon.

Suddenly to our amazement the grey sky parted, as cleanly as if it had been cut out with scissors and the shape of a red cross appeared. There was only the Cross. No shafts of light leading off from it, no indistinct edges so that sceptics might say it was a vague vision, it was as clear as if it had been a real one.

Then we remembered that it was the Eve of Whitsun, an appropriate time to see a Red Cross, but even more so when we learnt later that the British Forces in Crete and her naval warships round the island had suffered the most terrible casualties, when the Germans attacked from the air. I then came to see the meaning of my dream. 'Stukas will do it.'

We were lucky in getting a good summer that year. Not much of the proverbial rain the Lakes are famous for, so we could be out of doors a great deal. We explored the valley beyond Throstle Farm, as it was picturesquely called, and viewed the heights called Mockerkin where George Fox is said to have preached from the Crags, one can imagine the sturdy people from the neighbouring farms gathering after a long and arduous treck to this outlandish spot and listening with considerable interest to this magnetic speaker with an urgent message for humanity. 'I saw there was an ocean of darkness and death but an infinite ocean of light and love that flowed over the darkness.'

They would not be a meek audience and easy to convince of the goodness of God, since they had to face up to the forces of nature and cope with these on their own.

The Lakes are *not* dominated by titled landlords and there are no areas fenced off with notices 'Trespassers will be Prosecuted' as in 'the Dukeries'. Nor was there any feeling of living under the protection of an organised estate.

Much of it was wild land entirely unfenced, and the sturdy independence of the farmers was in many ways inspiring. They knew how to cope with problems and fend for themselves. Mockerkin was, as it were, the end of their kingdom; from its heights you looked down to Silloth and the waterway which divided them from Scotland, another land.

Because of the farming community being the mainstay of the village, any leisure activities seemed to take place on Monday, an unusual day but that was market day curiously enough in Cockermouth. We soon came to understand the practicality of this arrangement, because during the week everybody wore their old work-a-day clothes and concentrated on the job but on Monday you had to put on something better to go to town and spruce up generally and then it saved a lot of time and trouble to be dressed up for the evening activity too.

I don't recall that there was much going on in comparison with our mining parish in Staffordshire. Farming is a very largely individual occupation. Mining involves a whole community. There were Missionary Meetings, local Committee meetings for those who were permanent residents, and the W.I. which was of course particularly active in this county neighbourhood where recipes for home-made food and household methods were so important for a 'do it yourself' community.

One most important function was the painting of the Pace eggs in which our good friend, Mrs Fearon took a great pride creating such beautiful patterns. What is the origin of this strange custom which dates back so many years and which is so especially practised in Cumberland?

Food of course was all rationed any extras seemed very scarce, especially the vegetarian things that we liked. The Fearons had a very charming 'boarder' during the summer season, a huge foxhound called 'Steamer' of which we were very fond. He was well named because he sailed about imperturbably rather like a large ship, and one day he must have sailed into our friend Gladys's sitting room when she was not there, seized up an enormous packet of vegetarian fat called Nutta and then retired to the field prepared to enjoy it! Unfortunately he found it not at all to his taste and having made a good many dents in it with his mouth which put it out of the question for human consumption, left it out on the grass and sailed on. Imagine our dismay when we found it since food was so hard to replace in those days.

The summer went on, and no news came from Jordans of a house. Midsummer came. That was a day I recall well. We must have been for a morning walk and were just coming up the hall when the kitchen door flew open and out rushed the farmer's wife, Mrs Fearon, carrying in her hand a small wireless on which she had got the one o'clock news.

'Hitler's invaded Russia! Hitler's invaded Russia!' she cried.

We gasped with surprise and one might say relief for we had feared so much that he might choose our shores. We also received the news with special interest because it was almost exactly what our psychic friend Gladys had got clairvoyantly we had been told. 'At a time that you call Midsummer a step will be taken and you will look back and say 'This is the turning point in the war' and not only that, it will shape things after the war.' Those are the words we had received and they were fulfilled.

It was strange how after this dramatic announcement, things seemed to go back to normal and the great events on the Eastern Front became strangely remote. It was things that affected daily life on which we now placed most emphasis.

The summer went and the advancing autumn made the bracken turn an intense golden brown on the mountainside, especially when one viewed it from the back of the house. The mountain there had a strange gap in it, I suppose you would call it a pass. Somehow when you looked at it there was always a feeling of expectancy, as if someone would come riding through it.

The days were getting shorter, the nights longer. The paraffin was in short supply for the lamp. We went to bed early because of keeping warm and not using too much light and heat.

Then one day came a wire telling us a house was to let in Jordans. Would we take it? We wired back. 'Yes.' After that everything became a rush, packing up our belongings and the agony of deciding which of the cat colony on the farm we had become such friends with we would take with us to our new home. We decided on a dark tortoiseshell, 'Ma', whose pleading eyes we could not deny, and a very thin lively little dark tortoiseshell called Doodie, who had a tendency to asthma and needed a more sheltered life that she had then. Alas Ma, who was deaf, was run over by the grocer's lorry when delivering goods, and killed instantly so only Doodie came.

On a dark morning in the blackout, we were bundled into the local taxi with our luggage packed around us so tightly we could hardly move. Doodie was in a cat basket lent by the Vicar.

We had a long journey to the train at Penrith. Imagine our horror when on the road over the famous Moreland Shap the basket collapsed and we could feel Doodie streaking round us in the car, but every time we tried to grasp her in the complete dark she escaped. At last somehow we grabbed her and forced her back into the ruins of the basket. The train (the only one in the day) was coming in as we arrived and we tore across the bridge. A friendly porter proved a godsend by providing a sack into which we slipped the basket and the cat.

The stationmaster, seeing our distress, pushed us into a first class carriage where we sank down thankfully and remained there till we turned out in the urban environment of Watford where another taxi met us and drove us to our new home.

How different life was to be now at Jordans, knowing that the encircling darkness was not due to the simple domestic crisis of the paraffin running out in the lamp, but to the strictly enforced blackout for fear of enemy planes overhead. As Auntie Jones, a cheerful housekeeper at a neighbour's house, said, 'I don't mind when he is going over but I can't bear it when he's Hooverin'!'

Sometimes at night we could see the wicked glow from London on fire. My days were spent in London, bombs permitting, dealing with refugees from all over the world at Friends International Centre. Truly a wider sphere had opened now, far 'beyond the nursery window'.

McLEAN AT THE GOLDEN OWL
George Goodchild
Inspector McLean has resigned from Scotland Yard's CID and has opened an office in Wimpole Street. With the help of his able assistant, Tiny, he solves many crimes, including those of kidnapping, murder and poisoning.

KATE WEATHERBY
Anne Goring
Derbyshire, 1849: The Hunter family are the arrogant, powerful masters of Clough Grange. Their feuds are sparked by a generation of guilt, despair and ill-fortune. But their passions are awakened by the arrival of nineteen-year-old Kate Weatherby.

A VENETIAN RECKONING
Donna Leon
When the body of a prominent inter-national lawyer is found in the carriage of an intercity train, Commissario Guido Brunetti begins to dig deeper into the secret lives of the once great and good.

A TASTE FOR DEATH
Peter O'Donnell

Modesty Blaise and Willie Garvin take on impossible odds in the shape of Simon Delicata, the man with a taste for death, and Swordmaster, Wenczel, in a terrifying duel. Finally, in the Sahara desert, the intrepid pair must summon every killing skill to survive.

SEVEN DAYS FROM MIDNIGHT
Rona Randall

In the Comet Theatre, London, seven people have good reason for wanting beautiful Maxine Culver out of the way. Each one has reason to fear her blackmail. But whose shadow is it that lurks in the wings, waiting to silence her once and for all?

QUEEN OF THE ELEPHANTS
Mark Shand

Mark Shand knows about the ways of elephants, but he is no match for the tiny Parbati Barua, the daughter of India's greatest expert on the Asian elephant, the late Prince of Gauripur, who taught her everything. Shand sought out Parbati to take part in a film about the plight of the wild herds today in north-east India.

THE DARKENING LEAF
Caroline Stickland

On storm-tossed Chesil Bank in 1847, the young lovers, Philobeth and Frederick, prevent wreckers mutilating the apparent corpse of a young woman. Discovering she is still alive, Frederick takes her to his grandmother's home. But the rescue is to have violent and far-reaching effects . . .

A WOMAN'S TOUCH
Emma Stirling

When Fenn went to stay on her uncle's farm in Africa, the lovely Helena Starr seemed to resent her — especially when Dr Jason Kemp agreed to Fenn helping in his bush hospital. Though it seemed Jason saw Fenn as little more than a child, her feelings for him were those of a woman.

A DEAD GIVEAWAY
Various Authors

This book offers the perfect opportunity to sample the skills of five of the finest writers of crime fiction — Clare Curzon, Gillian Linscott, Peter Lovesey, Dorothy Simpson and Margaret Yorke.

DOUBLE INDEMNITY — MURDER FOR INSURANCE
Jad Adams

This is a collection of true cases of murderers who insured their victims then killed them — or attempted to. Each tense, compelling account tells a story of cold-blooded plotting and elaborate deception.

THE PEARLS OF COROMANDEL
By Keron Bhattacharya

John Sugden, an ambitious young Oxford graduate, joins the Indian Civil Service in the early 1920s and goes to uphold the British Raj. But he falls in love with a young Hindu girl and finds his loyalties tragically divided.

WHITE HARVEST
Louis Charbonneau

Kathy McNeely, a marine biologist, sets out for Alaska to carry out important research. But when she stumbles upon an illegal ivory poaching operation that is threatening the world's walrus population, she soon realises that she will have to survive more than the harsh elements . . .

TO THE GARDEN ALONE
Eve Ebbett

Widow Frances Morley's short, happy marriage was childless, and in a succession of borders she attempts to build a substitute relationship for the husband and family she does not have. Over all hovers the shadow of the man who terrorized her childhood.

CONTRASTS
Rowan Edwards

Julia had her life beautifully planned — she was building a thriving pottery business as well as sharing her home with her friend Pippa, and having fun owning a goat. But the goat's problems brought the new local vet, Sebastian Trent, into their lives.

MY OLD MAN AND THE SEA
David and Daniel Hays

Some fathers and sons go fishing together. David and Daniel Hays decided to sail a tiny boat seventeen thousand miles to the bottom of the world and back. Together, they weave a story of travel, adventure, and difficult, sometimes terrifying, sailing.

SQUEAKY CLEAN
James Pattinson

An important attribute of a prospective candidate for the United States presidency is not to have any dirt in your background which an eager muckraker can dig up. Senator William S. Gallicauder appeared to fit the bill perfectly. But then a skeleton came rattling out of an English cupboard.

NIGHT MOVES
Alan Scholefield

It was the first case that Macrae and Silver had worked on together. Malcolm Underdown had brutally stabbed to death Edward Craig and had attempted to murder Craig's fiancée, Jane Harrison. He swore he would be back for her. Now, four years later, he has simply walked from the mental hospital. Macrae and Silver must get to him — before he gets to Jane.

GREATEST CAT STORIES
Various Authors

Each story in this collection is chosen to show the cat at its best. James Herriot relates a tale about two of his cats. Stella Whitelaw has written a very funny story about a lion. Other stories provide examples of courageous, clever and lucky cats.